SOMETHING LOST

FUNERALS AND WEDDINGS ~ BOOK ONE

BERNADETTE MARIE

5 PRINCE PUBLISHING

Published by 5 PRINCE PUBLISHING

PO Box 865, Arvada, CO 80001

www.5PrinceBooks.com

ISBN digital: 978-1-63112-265-1

ISBN print: 978-1-63112-324-5

Cover Credit: Marianne Nowicki

To Stan,
For accepting every single, solitary flaw
I have as a strength.
You are my sun, from which, hangs the moon.
I love you, forever and a day!

ACKNOWLEDGMENTS

To my own Fab Five: You hang the moon.

To my mom and sister: There is no better duo I'd rather take "traumas" and turn them into successes with.

To Cate: I am extremely happy that you continue to be part of my team and make me look good.

To My Book Hive: Thank you too for helping me create amazing works of art.

To My Readers: Thank you for your positive feedback and love, which makes me want to continue to create these amazing characters.

To anyone who seeks out professional help in times of need, I salute you. To anyone who seeks out a friendly ear to listen to their problems, or who journals to get the demons out of your head and onto a page, I admire your strength. To anyone who chooses the path of therapist, doctor, counsellor, or clergy with the intent to be that help when sought after, you have my utmost respect.

Mental Health should be a priority for every person! Take the time to listen to yourself, and put mental health care into your routine. Reach out if you need help from others. Be a shoulder if someone needs it.

ALSO BY BERNADETTE MARIE

THE MATCHMAKER SERIES

Matchmakers

Encore

Finding Hope

THE THREE MRS. MONROES TRILOGY

Amelia

Penelope

Vivian

THE ASPEN CREEK SERIES

First Kiss

Unexpected Admirer

On Thin Ice

Indomitable Spirit

THE DENVER BRIDE SERIES

Cart Before the Horse

Never Saw it Coming

Candy Kisses

ROMANTIC SUSPENSE

Chasing Shadows

PARANORMAL ROMANCES

The Tea Shop

The Last Goodbye

HOLIDAY FAVORITES

Corporate Christmas

Tropical Christmas

THE DEVEREAUX FAMILY SERIES

Kennedy Devereaux

Chase Devereaux

Max Devereaux

Paige Devereaux

FUNERALS AND WEDDINGS SERIES

Something Lost

Something Discovered

Something Found

Something Forbidden

Something New

SOMETHING LOST

CHAPTER 1

The thought crossed his mind, had he ever been to a funeral when it wasn't snowing or raining?

Craig stepped out of his car, opened the back door, and pulled out his overcoat. Shrugging it on over his suit, he buttoned it up and adjusted his scarf. Cars pulled into the lot and he watched as others followed the same routine he did to ward off the cold that nipped at him.

"Hey, Turner!"

Craig turned at the calling out of his last name. A smile came to his lips as Raymond Stewart maneuvered between the cars and headed toward him.

There were no handshakes. Each of the men opened their arms and embraced the other.

"It is so good to see you," Ray said as he pulled back and scanned a look over Craig.

"What a crappy reason to get together."

"What an honor though, huh? After all these years, and they ask us to be his pallbearers?"

"I'm not going to lie. I was a bit surprised to get his son's email," Craig admitted.

"No matter what ever happened between all of us, and the other players that came and went, the five of us had a bond with him. I can't help but think we were replacements for Theo—we'll you know, maybe we dulled his pain some?"

Craig wasn't so sure about that. How did a man ever get over the loss of a child?

He tucked his hands into the pockets of his coat and pulled out the gloves he'd stored there. Slipping his hands into the lined leather, he watched his breath carry on the cold air.

"When was the last time you talked to him?" Craig asked as he nodded toward the hearse.

Ray tucked his gloved hands into the pockets of his coat as a frigid breeze blew between them. "Christmas card each year. His son got him on Facebook, so I chatted with him a few times there. Otherwise, I don't know when I actually spoke to him other than at my wedding."

Craig caught the sadness that flashed in Ray's eyes. "I heard about your divorce. I'm sorry, man."

"Shit happens, right? It was a good eight years, and a few really bad ones. But we work well together when it comes to the kids, and that's the most important part." Ray pulled his sunglasses down off his head and slid them on his face. "When did you talk to him last?"

Craig noticed they were taking the casket out of the hearse and carrying it inside the church through the side door. He gave Ray's question some thought.

"He got me my first sub job after college at a high school where he knew the staff pretty well. Gave me some recommendations over the years. Christmas card each year. I guess I didn't talk to him too much at all. I should have tried harder."

"He wouldn't have expected it. His job was to coach basketball and send us on our way."

Craig had thought about that too. Maybe that was the man's purpose in his life. Coach had given him skills to advance in the sport he loved, but he'd also helped him grow into the man he'd become. Coach Diaz didn't have to go above and beyond, but he had, even when Craig crossed the line and dated Coach's daughter, against his wishes. The man could have thrown in the towel and kicked him off the team. Instead, Coach Diaz helped Craig establish his career.

That was why Craig was there. He owed it to the man who didn't hold grudges and had continued to care for him, even if Craig had broken his daughter's heart.

"Look what crawls out of the gutters when there's a wedding or a funeral," the voice came from behind them. Craig and Ray turned to see Charlottender Burke, Bruce Griffin, and Toby Maxwell all walking their way.

It had been Alex that had called out to them and reached them before the others. He pulled Craig in for a hug, and then did the same to Ray. "Damn, it's been forever," he said as he slid his sunglasses to the top of his head.

Bruce and Toby greeted them in the same way, and then the five of them stood in a small circle. Awkward silence had fallen between them before Toby spoke.

"I can't believe Coach is gone. The memories, huh?"

They all agreed, nodding their heads.

Bruce tucked his hands into the pockets of his coat. "This is like old times. *The Fabulous Five* back together."

"Except our hair is different," Craig joked and they all laughed. "But it's good to see you guys. Maybe after the funeral we can catch up."

Alex nodded. "My flight doesn't leave until tomorrow."

"Why don't we all drive to the cemetery together, and then from there we'll go somewhere. I'll drive and bring you all back here when we're done."

Ray slapped a hand on Craig's shoulder. "That sounds like a plan."

"Craig?" This time when his name was called out, it was a

woman's voice. He turned to see Coach Diaz's daughter, Rachel, standing near the family car.

He turned his back on his friends and walked toward her.

She was bundled up in a long wool coat, a scarf tied around her neck, and that long dark hair pulled back in a ponytail.

"Rachel, I'm so sorry about your dad," he said as he leaned in and had kissed her on the cheek before he thought better of it. She was probably married, and now he'd crossed another line.

"Thank you. I'm pleased that you all came for the funeral and agreed to be pallbearers. It would mean a lot to him."

Craig studied her dark eyes, which hinted that they'd been filled with tears not too long before she'd called his name.

"It's our honor. He meant a lot to all of us too. Though we should have kept in better touch."

Rachel reached out and rested her gloved hand on his arm. "He kept tabs on you all, his Fabulous Five," she said with a smile as she used his name for them. "He was proud of everything you've done," she said and now Craig could feel the sting of tears forming in his eyes.

"Wow," he said blowing out a breath. "That means a lot."

"I have to go inside. Hal will walk you all through the process. I'll see you at the cemetery too."

"Yeah. We're going to drive together and then go somewhere and catch up."

Rachel's rosebud lips turned up into a smile. "That would make Dad happy, to know he brought you all back together again." She retracted her hand and slid it into the pocket of her coat. "I have to get inside. I'll get your number later. Maybe we could catch up."

A knot formed in his stomach. "I'd like that."

Rachel turned back and headed toward the side entrance of the church when another man moved in next to her and slid his arm around her as they disappeared inside.

4

"She's still into you," Ray said as they all walked up behind Craig.

"She's in mourning."

"Statement stands. I think this could be an interesting weekend." Ray put his arm around Craig's shoulders and the five friends walked into the church to say goodbye to the man who had made them a team.

CHAPTER 2

Coach Diaz had touched many lives, Craig thought as he sat down in the pew, his four best friends from college next to him. Coach's family in the center pews next to them.

Hal, Coach's son, had led them to their pew and let them know that they would only need to help with the casket at the cemetery. They'd each shook his hand and thanked him for thinking of them. Then the five of them sat at the front of the church as the service started.

There were other faces in the church that he recognized. Catherine Anderson, Rachel's best friend, had caught his eye as she looked around at those who had gathered. She offered him a smile and turned her attention back to the front of the church.

The ceremony highlighted Coach Diaz's life. A slideshow had been put together showing him from childhood through his last days. There, in the middle, were the photos of the teams he had coached through the years, including photos of Craig and his friends holding up trophies and banners, and even Coach Diaz on their shoulders. As the clip played, it warranted a chuckle from those in attendance.

It hadn't gone unnoticed by any of them that Rachel and her mother both turned to look at them when the slide had come up. Perhaps their time with the coach had meant more to him than Craig had even known. Maybe Ray had been right. They had been the team with Coach when his son had died, and they had rallied around him and his family. They'd won the championship that year too. Was that how Coach had managed? Were they a part of his recovery?

The five of them were a constant during those pivotal years. Craig swallowed hard. He really should have stayed in touch with the man.

When the sermon had concluded, the family rose, walked past the casket and out of the church. Each row was then escorted out of the pew and filed past the open casket.

The last row to file out was Craig's.

He and his pals stood shoulder to shoulder looking down at the man who was small and silver haired. His hands rested on his stomach. On one hand he had his wedding ring, on the other the matching championship ring that each of the men looking at him had tucked away in drawers. Craig drew in a breath. If it had meant so much to Coach to be buried with that ring, he'd sure as hell go home and find his own.

They all stood over the casket in silence. Was he supposed to say something to him, Craig wondered? Could he quietly put his message of thanks out into the universe?

Toby put his hand on Craig's shoulder. "What a man. A dad to us all. God's team is sure to win now."

Craig chuckled, but yeah, that's what he'd been thinking too.

RACHEL CLIMBED into the family limousine as people began to emerge from the church. Her mother and brother had gone back through the side door so they could say goodbye to her father one more time before they closed the casket.

She didn't want to see him again, not the way he was. She wanted to remember him full of life, and not still and cold.

As the church emptied out, and people walked to their cars, she watched as Craig and his friends walked out into the frozen air. Each of them slid on their sunglasses and stuck their hands into the pockets of their coats. Then, as Craig had mentioned they would, they all walked toward his car and climbed inside.

It had been ten years since she'd seen him last. Just as she'd told him, her father kept tabs on his champion boys, and he always shared that news with her.

What she and Craig had shared so many years ago was young, hot, and against her father's rules. She'd been eighteen the year he turned twenty-one, but she'd had eyes on the six-foot-two center since she'd been fifteen, and all but a fly on the wall around the college basketball team her father coached. Because her mother traveled extensively and her brother was in the Air Force, she spent a lot of time with her father and younger brother on campus. The older she got, the more wanted to be around Craig Turner.

She rested her head against the back of the seat as she watched her mother and brother emerge from the church. Her brother Hal had his arm around their sobbing mother.

Rachel scooted over so that her mother could climb in next to her. Immediately her mother took her hand and gave it a squeeze. "That's it," she sobbed. "We'll never see his face again."

Rachel wrapped her arm around her mother's shoulders and let her weep.

When her father's casket had been loaded back into the hearse, Hal joined them in the car, dressed in his officers' uniform, Rachel thought he was the spitting image of photos she'd seen of their father at that age.

Soon the hearse began to pull away from the church, and their car followed. Rachel could see the cars in the parking lot turn on their lights and form a line behind them. Every person was thinking about them, she knew, and it was an odd feeling to be on everyone's mind. Maybe it was because she knew it was temporary.

Tomorrow, everyone who came out to celebrate her father would return to their lives. He'd be a memory that would come up from time to time, and perhaps someday they'd forget him.

The thought stung, because she knew that her father had never forgotten anyone, and that was part of what had made him such an incredible teacher and coach.

When she thought about her father doing the things he loved in life, her mind wandered to Craig. She knew he'd become a teacher, just as he'd planned to do. He'd even coached high school basketball.

When her father found his boys, as he'd call them, on Facebook, he friended each of them.

Of course, they friended him back and her father made it a point to show her what each of them had been up to.

At the time, Craig was married, and though he and Rachel had never been as serious as she might have thought at eighteen, it had broken her heart to see pictures of him in a tuxedo next to the beautiful blonde in her wedding dress. She never friended him herself, but it hadn't stopped her from googling his name or checking his profile over the years. Three days earlier, when he'd accepted the invitation to be a pallbearer, he'd posted a photo of the two of them. He had written a moving tribute to her father and tagged him in it. When Rachel had read it, alone in her tiny house, she had sobbed until Rover, her teacup poodle, settled into her lap to calm her.

Now, she knew, Craig was teaching at a community college and was no longer married to the blonde.

CHAPTER 3

The men stepped out of Craig's Acura, and pulled their coats tighter as a breeze had picked up at the cemetery. The cold had Craig's teeth chattering.

The hearse door was open. Craig and the others moved to the car. Hal thanked each of them again, as they all got into place and carried the man, who had been a father figure to them all, to the site where he would be buried.

The crowd walked over the frozen ground to the canopy that had been set up. Family sat in the chairs next to the grave, and the mourners gathered around them. The pallbearers lifted the casket into place, and then took their places among the mourners, and Hal with the family. They all moved in close to one another and Craig wondered how much of that was to keep warm.

Words were spoken and prayers said. He watched as Rachel's arm came to her mother's shoulders and their heads pressed together. Craig couldn't imagine the pain. He'd never lost a parent or a sibling, and Rachel had already lost both a brother and now a father.

When the small service at the grave had concluded, the crowd formed around the family to extend their condolences. Craig and the others seemed to hover toward the back of the line, but soon, he was face to face with Rachel again, and her mother and brother.

"Mom," Rachel began, "Do you remember Craig Turner?"

"Oh, Craig," Coach Diaz's wife placed her gloved hands on both sides of his face and pulled him down to her so she could kiss his cheeks. She looked at the men who followed behind him. "His team. You're his team," she repeated.

"We were that, ma'am. He was a fine man. He helped me become the man I am today," Craig said, and he meant every word.

"He loved you all as if you were his own. Especially after Theo —" she stopped and Craig couldn't help but pull her into him.

"HE WAS A GOOD MAN," Craig whispered in Mrs. Diaz's ear as he eased back.

He shifted a look toward Rachel who batted tears away with long, dark lashes.

Each of the men behind him, hugged Rachel and her mother, then shook Hal's hand. Craig took a moment to walk away from the grave and the people to collect himself. Being reminded of Theo seemed to have deepened the pain he was feeling.

"That meant a lot to her, that you all came," Rachel's voice came from behind him and he turned to see her standing there. Her nose red from the cold and the tears that had wiped away her makeup.

"I feel guilty that I didn't remain closer to him. Hell, I only live twenty miles away."

"We all were meant to go our own ways. He knew that." Rachel pulled her phone from her pocket and handed it to Craig. "Will you put your number in here? I was serious. I want to catch up."

Craig took the phone with its glittery pink case, which he thought fit the woman in front of him. He plugged in his name and number, even adding his email, for good measure, he supposed. He handed it back to her and she slid it into her pocket.

"It was really good to see you," she said, and he swore those dark eyes grew darker.

"You too. Call me whenever," he added.

"I will."

He watched as she walked away, passing the guys as they walked toward him, even touching Alex's arm as she passed.

Bruce turned toward him. "He's not even in the ground, and you're making moves on his daughter again?"

Craig chuckled. "She asked for my number. She wants to catch up."

Toby hummed. "I'll bet she does. You never forget your first," he teased, and Craig took the jab. "I'm starving. Where are you taking us?"

Craig thought for a moment. "Get back to the car. I know a place."

The five of them walked through the cemetery, past the grave of Coach Diaz, and his family who still spoke with those who had gathered. Craig exchanged glances with Rachel one more time before he continued on.

Surely she just wanted to catch up, just like she said she did. It had been ten years, and hadn't they both grown up?

But in their time, they had caused each other a lot of pain, and Coach Diaz, too. The fact that the man continued to vouch for him as a teacher and a man, well, it always surprised him. Craig had broken his rules, gotten caught, and done it again. The innocence of youth, he supposed. It made you stupid and still likable. It brought out the worst in you, and changed you. It made you have to grow up, but was never something you forgot.

Craig laughed when he looked up toward his car and saw Ray

and Alex sprinting toward it, both reaching for the passenger door. Two grown men pushing the other out of the way and laughing.

Then, sometimes when you were with the right people, he thought, the innocence of youth, and the stupidity of it all, could come flooding back and feel like a warm blanket.

CHAPTER 4

Craig parked his car next to the Platte River and laughed when Alex looked around.

"Are you kidding me? You're parking your car here?" he said with panic laced words.

"You haven't been here in a long time. This is the hip and upcoming neighborhood," Craig assured him and the others in the back laughed. "Seriously, this place is filled with millennials and their pets living in overpriced studio apartments. It's not the same Denver you left, my friend."

They all climbed from the car and headed to the brewery on the corner. When they were seated, they each ordered a specialty beer from the ever-changing menu.

"What was this place?" Alex asked.

Bruce shook his head. "Can't even remember. Plumbing parts, or something like that."

"And there's a grocery store on the corner? Wasn't that an old car lot where they sold stolen cars?"

They all laughed, but Alex was right. That's what had sat on that corner for as long as Craig could remember.

When the beers were delivered to the table, each of them held their glasses up.

"To Coach," Bruce said. "We should hope to be half the man he was."

They all agreed and tapped glasses, saluting the man who had meant so much to them.

Food was ordered, and the men sat back to enjoy one another's company and get caught up on old times.

They all still lived in Colorado, except for Alex, who had moved to the east coast shortly after graduation, and currently lived in Boston. The razzing that had ensued after he had said be-ah, instead of beer, had taken them all back to the dorm rooms they'd once gathered in.

Alex and Bruce had been friends since childhood, having been in the same class at some high-priced private school, in the high-end Cherry Creek area since they were in kindergarten. They were roommates in college and across the hall from Craig and Ray, who had gone to the same high school and been on the same basketball team. Toby, who had originally come from Texas, had the room next to Craig and Ray all to himself. They'd called him spoiled, but it had made for a much better opportunity to party.

Toby rested his arm on the back of his chair and looked around the table. "I can't believe we haven't done this in years. When was the last time we got together like this?"

They all gave it some thought as they sipped their beers. Alex set his glass down first. "When my dad died. Four years ago. I came back when he was sick, and you all came to the funeral. We did this then."

The mood had grown somber. Craig nodded. "We have to plan this out better," he teased and it warranted a few weak chuckles.

"We do need to," Alex agreed. "Actually, you all suck if you don't do this more often. I live on the other end of the country.

Each of you are no more than forty-five minutes away from one another."

Craig sipped his beer. He was right. They all sucked.

He and Ray would catch dinner once in a while, or even a Nuggets game if it worked out. He'd cross paths with Bruce on occasion and they'd catch up. Toby always did his own thing, and Craig couldn't remember when he'd hung out with him last, though they exchanged emails and texts often.

Their food arrived, and their beer was refilled.

Alex sat back and studied them all. "So, Craig is divorced and teaching community college."

"You're hitting all of my highlights, pal," Craig smirked.

"Toby, what the hell, you just work all the time?"

Toby gave him a slow nod. "Married to the job, man. But would you like to see my house in Boulder?" He winked and it got a laugh.

Craig had seen the monstrosity that Toby talked about. Six-bedroom house, game room, industrial sized kitchen with state of the art appliances, and a heated outdoor pool all backed up to the Flatirons. And he lived there alone. It was the most impressively sad thing Craig had ever seen.

Alex turned his attention to Bruce. "And what about you? What are you doing these days?"

Bruce bit the meat off a chicken wing, discarded the bone, and wiped his fingers and mouth with his napkin. He took a sip from his beer, and then made eye contact with each of the men around him.

"Currently looking for a job," he said with a hint of embarrassment. "Haven't had steady work in six months."

The air in the room was thicker, Craig noticed. And he knew each of them was trying to think of something they could do to help.

Bruce lifted his beer in salute toward Alex. "I'll bet you're extremely glad I never married your sister now, aren't you?"

There was a flash of annoyance in Alex's eyes over the statement. The two of them had gone to blows more than once over Bruce's interest in Alex's younger sister. But Alex grinned.

"She's done worse, but you're still off the table."

Bruce laughed at that, sipped his beer, and set it down. "I have a lead on a job in the Springs. Military civilian job. Who knows?"

Alex turned his attention to Ray. "How's Kelly?"

Ray winced, and so had Craig. He'd felt the conversation coming. He knew it would be coming for himself, next.

Ray eased back in his chair. "She's doing great. She's living in the house I worked my ass off to buy, but she's keeping the kids safe and happy." There was a bite in his words as his lips pursed. "I'm living in a shitty rental about six miles from them. I get the kids every other week, and I'm still busting my ass with all the new housing developments going in around the city."

Alex leaned in on his forearms. "Man, I didn't know. I'm sorry."

"It's still a little fresh. Time cures everything, right?"

For a moment they'd grown silent again, each taking a sip from their beer. Then, all eyes turned to Craig.

"Not much to say here," he said, sitting back in surrender. "You all know I'm divorced. Didn't even make three years. I'm teaching at Red Rocks Community College and haven't tossed a basketball through a net in years."

Now they laughed.

Bruce lifted his beer. "We should change that before Alex goes back. YMCA, tomorrow. Two o'clock?"

Craig lifted his glass. "I'm in."

"I'm in," Alex agreed, and Ray and Toby followed.

Toby finished his beer and patted Alex on the shoulder. "Your turn, big guy. What have you been up to since you were here last?"

Alex's eyes grew darker, and he bit down on his lip. "Not

18

much. I was in a relationship, but that ended months ago. She was having a lot of relationships, but living with me."

Toby winced. "Ouch."

"Yeah. Had a few months where I might have been drunk the whole time. Cost me my career I'd worked so damn hard for, but hey," he shifted his attention to Bruce, "we land on our feet, right?"

Bruce lifted his glass in salute. "Damn straight. We all do."

CHAPTER 5

C raig kicked his feet up on the footstool in front of his couch and aimed the remote control at the TV. A grin formed on his lips. When he'd gotten up that morning, and shrugged on that black suit, he'd never have imagined that the day would have turned out to have been good for his soul.

Though he was sad that Coach had died, Craig was glad he'd been there to pay his last respects. Having all the boys together, that had been a blessing he hadn't expected.

It wasn't as if he'd thought they wouldn't show for the funeral, but he simply hadn't given it much thought at all. And to see that Alex had flown in from Boston, that made it even more special.

Craig lifted the bottle of beer he'd held in his hand to his lips. He and the boys had spent hours talking and catching up. They'd each had their highs and their lows, but together they could laugh about it. It did appear that none of them had been lucky in love, though most of them had started that way.

As he flipped through the channels, he landed on a rerun of an SNL skit from the late seventies, and stopped. No one was better than Belushi and Ackroyd.

For some reason the SNL flashback had Craig thinking of

Rachel Diaz and late nights at Coach's house with the team. They'd play stupid board games until the wee hours of the morning in his game room in the basement, and watch late night TV. They never stayed the night, but Craig assumed that having all the boys on the team at Coach's house, under his supervision, kept them out of trouble and bonded them. And now he knew, keeping them close filled the hole that losing Theo had created.

He'd heard that it wasn't like that anymore. Teams couldn't have anything to do with the coach outside of team time. That was too bad, but he understood it. Too many coaches had abused that privilege. But for Craig and the other guys, Coach was a father figure, a mentor, a counselor, and a friend.

And, Craig thought as he lifted the bottle to his lips again, it hadn't hurt that he had a daughter that kept Craig's interest.

It had been nice to see her again, though he'd wished it were under better circumstances.

Sipping from his beer, he thought about Rachel. She hadn't changed at all. Her dark hair was pulled back, but he vividly knew what it looked like when it cascaded over her shoulders. Those dark eyes, though sad when they'd spoken, were warm and could see right through him—he'd felt it.

Craig had been lucky to hear a word she'd said to him. Beyond his grief, he'd also been caught up in watching those rosebud lips move as she spoke.

He blew out a breath and finished his beer.

There had been many nights in college that he'd lost sleep over the young woman who had once been nothing more than a younger sister to them all. But there had come a day that she wasn't a young girl anymore, and she'd caught Craig's attention.

Craig set his bottle on the table next to his couch and rested his head back. Since Craig had graduated, he hadn't seen Rachel. But even marriage hadn't kept her from creeping into his mind.

Now, he knew, he wouldn't sleep a full night again since she'd asked for his number and mentioned that she wanted to catch up.

~

RACHEL SAT in her quiet kitchen, the only light on was the one over the sink. She held a bag of frozen peas over her eyes to help reduce the puffiness caused by crying, and let the silence surround her.

When she'd woken that morning, she was sure she wouldn't shed any tears. From the moment her father had become sick, nearly four months earlier, she had shed enough tears that she was sure she was dry. The planning for his funeral and the funeral itself was business. She was her mother's caretaker, and her brother was tending to most of the last minute details. They had promised each other that they would take care of their mother, and they were focused on that task.

Hal had decided to stay the rest of the weekend with their mother, and had sent Rachel home.

She was grateful to have some down time, but the moment she'd opened her front door, the emotions and the exhaustion mixed. For the past six hours, she hadn't stopped crying, and now her head throbbed, and her eyes stung.

Rachel lowered the bag of peas and picked up her mug of tea. She took a careful sip and let out a sigh. The dreaded day had come and gone, and now it was over.

She closed her eyes and thought about the people that had been at the funeral. The church had been at capacity. Her father had touched the lives of the entire community, and beyond.

The tears threatened again when she thought about seeing the boys—men—her father thought so much of.

Wiping away the tears, she picked up her phone and scrolled through her contacts until she came upon Craig's name.

Rachel's hand shook just looking at his number on her phone. Did she have the guts to really call him and catch up, just as she'd said she wanted to? Was it even worth it, to dredge up old memories?

Her father had loved Craig like a son, and he'd forgiven them both for their brief relationship, which was against his rules. Perhaps it was just better to let the past be the past and move on.

But she didn't want to.

There hadn't been a day when he hadn't crossed her mind in the past ten years.

It's Rachel, she typed onto the screen. *Can we meet this week and catch up?*

CHAPTER 6

Craig looked at the message on his phone, his finger hovering over the keyboard as he formulated his reply.

Did he ask her to dinner? Should they meet for drinks? Would it be best if he simply replied with a *sure*? He was at a loss for words.

She'd asked for his number so they could catch up, but honestly, he hadn't expected to hear from her. And even if she was going to reach out, he hadn't expected her to do so on the day she buried her father.

With his fingers still not moving, he watched as the set of blinking dots appeared, telling him she was sending a new message.

Lunch tomorrow? One o'clock?

Craig smiled at her response. She'd usually been the forward one while he tended to be rendered speechless by her. He began his reply and then erased it with a wince. He already had plans.

Playing ball with the guys at two. How about dinner at seven? I'll come your way, he replied.

Juanita's by Flatirons Mall. Half way.

Craig smiled down at her response, and before he could confirm, a photo came through.

He turned his phone to see himself and the boys with Coach. It had to be their freshman year, they all looked so young. He remembered the picture, and the barbecue in Coach's back yard. Standing next to Coach was a young Rachel.

Craig blew out a breath. He would have been almost nineteen in the picture and that would have made her fifteen. In the years that followed, she blossomed into a strong and beautiful woman, but then, she was just a kid. Hell, he was just a kid.

Now, they were adults, he in his thirties. And to think, everything ten years earlier seemed so important.

Are we on? she sent through another message and he realized he'd been fixated on the picture.

Yeah. I'll be there. I look forward to seeing you, he added.

She sent a heart and a smiley face. *Me too.*

CRAIG TIGHTENED the laces on his shoes as he sat court-side for the first time in years. Alex walked through the door with his sister, Sarah.

"We had an odd number, so I brought the next best thing," he teased as Sarah set her gym bag down next to Craig.

"He thinks by bringing me, you'll all take it easy," Sarah admitted as she pulled her high tops from the bag.

"Take it easy?" Craig laughed. "You were better than all of us combined."

"I know that," she said with a wink.

Before she could toe off her winter boots, Bruce moved in behind her with a big bear hug, lifting her off her feet.

"Damn I missed you," he said lowering her to the ground, spinning her toward him, and kissing her loudly on the cheek.

Sarah laughed easily as she placed her hands on Bruce's chest, and Craig watched the entire scene play out. Was she clueless? Bruce had longed for her since they were kids, but he was sure Sarah had never had any idea.

He'd heard the conversations between Alex and Bruce for years. Bruce would make a comment about Alex's sexy sister, and Alex would come uncorked. Craig was never sure if it was just banter or if Alex was actually willing to kick Bruce's ass for his sister's honor.

"Hands off," Alex yelled across the court. "I didn't bring her so you could put your paws on her."

Craig finished tying his shoes and Sarah sat down next to him.

"I haven't seen you in ages," she said. "How's the wife?"

Craig shook his head and chuckled. "You really haven't seen me in ages have you? Haven't been married for years."

Sarah turned her head toward him and her brows drew together. "He's an asshole. You'd think he'd tell me things like that before I jumped into seeing you all again and make a jerk of myself."

She was just one of the guys, he remembered. Her language, her skill on the court, and if memory served, she could drink them all under the table.

"Eh, I don't talk about it much. We weren't married long enough for it to even count." The worst part was, he believed that. Why had they even bothered?

Sarah slipped on her shoes, tied them, and jumped up from her seat. "Okay, so who wants to win?"

Bruce was quick to wrap his arm around her shoulders. "I take you," he said narrowing his gaze on Alex. "C'mon, Craig, join us and we will kick their asses."

Alex shook his head. "You are such a child."

Craig stood, kicking his bag under the bench. "Just don't mess up my face. I have a dinner date."

The five others on the court stopped and turned to him. Toby dribbled the ball. "One day after the funeral and you have a date with Coach's daughter?"

"I didn't say that."

"You didn't have to," Toby said as he threw the ball in Craig's direction. "How'd you score that?"

"She asked."

Ray took the ball from Craig, looking him straight in the eye. "You don't really want to get involved, do you?" he said in a hushed tone. "C'mon, you made a promise to the man."

"I broke that promise already."

Ray nodded. "One dinner?"

"One dinner."

"I doubt that," Ray said, and took the ball to the center of the court.

Craig set his jaw. Leave it to Ray to bring up the past in a way that made Craig second guess everything.

Yeah, he'd made a promise to Coach to stay away from his daughter, and he hadn't. Then, he'd made another promise to him to stay away from her, and he hadn't. Craig blew out a breath, maybe dinner was a bad idea. What if Rachel didn't want to catch up? What if she wanted to tell him what a piece of crap he was for pursuing her all those years ago? Then again, maybe she wanted give him a hard time over not keeping in touch. After all, she was every bit as guilty when it came to them breaking all of Coach's rules. He hadn't done it alone.

He was pulled from his thoughts when the basketball ricocheted off his arm, and Bruce caught it when it bounced.

"Get your head in the game, Turner. We have some ass to kick."

CHAPTER 7

Rachel watched as her mother stirred stew around in her bowl. Her eyes were dark and sunken, and Rachel was sure she hadn't slept in a week.

"Aren't you going to eat?" her mother asked her as she stirred her bowl as well.

"I have dinner plans, so I don't want to eat too much."

She received the reaction she'd been prepared for. Her mother pushed away her bowl and her shoulders dropped.

"You have a date?"

"I have dinner plans," Rachel corrected. "It's not a date."

Her mother nodded. Hal had dinner plans too. There had been a lot of people who had come to her father's funeral from out of town, and it was understood that they'd all catch up with them. But in the moment, Rachel felt small.

"I can come back when I'm done, and stay," she offered.

Her mother pulled her bowl back to her and took a bite of the stew. "I'll be okay. You forget, I was alone a lot when I traveled for business, and then your father was on the road coaching and you both had moved out. I can take care of myself."

"No doubt," Rachel said as she stood and carried her bowl to the sink to dispose of the stew she'd taken to appease her mother. "If you change your mind, let me know. I don't expect to be more than an hour or so."

Her mother nodded. "Who are you having dinner with?"

This would be a good time to lie to her mother, Rachel thought as she loaded the bowl into the dishwasher. But she wouldn't. Her mother liked Craig, so had her father, but it would warrant a reaction.

"I'm having dinner with Craig Turner."

Her mother lowered her spoon back to the bowl. "Oh. He asked you to dinner on the day after we buried your father?"

There was the accusing tone. Rachel was woman enough to admit the truth to her.

"I asked him to dinner."

"Moving right along," her mother scooped up a spoonful of stew and dropped it back into the bowl.

"It's not like that." Rachel sat back down in the chair she'd earlier vacated, and reached for her mother's hand. "I'm not seeing him. I asked him to dinner to catch up. I haven't seen him in ten years. He's a good man. He's always been a good man, and you know that."

Her mother worried her lip. "Your father asked you not to see him."

"You're right. And as an adult, I understand why. As an eighteen-year-old girl, I didn't."

Tears welled in her mother's eyes. "He caused you a lot of pain, baby. Why would you want to go through that again?"

"I'm not going to go through it. He has no idea he caused me anything. Mama, I'm a grown woman. I'm educated. I'm successful. Any misstep in my life hasn't hindered me. I need a few moments with him to ease an ache in my heart. Craig Turner is a good man. Daddy always thought so."

"And his wife is okay with you having dinner with him?"

A smile tugged at Rachel's mouth, but she fought it back. "He's not married anymore."

Her mother's eyes went dark again. "Oh. That's good for you."

Rachel rose and pressed a kiss to her mother's cheek. She would worry forever, Rachel knew, especially when it came to Craig Turner. But Rachel wasn't worried about how he would treat her. He'd never been anything but a gentleman and careful lover.

Her heart beat faster when she thought of him that way. This was just a casual dinner, she reminded herself. Craig was forever off limits.

RACHEL PULLED into the parking lot and searched for the Acura she'd seen Craig drive away in at her father's funeral. When she found it, she pulled in next to it and parked.

Flipping up the mirror on the back of her visor, she gave herself one last look. Her eyes were still red from days of tears, but she looked okay with a little makeup and her hair done in curls. Pulling her lipgloss from the cup holder, she opened it and ran the wand over her lips. That would help.

She closed the gloss, dropped it back in the cup holder, and grabbed her purse before opening the door and stepping out into the frigid February night air.

He was waiting for her by the door, in the long wool coat he'd worn to her father's funeral the day before. His six-foot-two always seemed taller to her when he was dressed up.

The closer Rachel got to him, the harder her heart hammered in her chest. "Thanks for meeting me," she said as she neared him.

"I was happy to get the invitation."

"How was your game with the guys?"

"Sarah was our ringer, and she kicked our asses."

That caused Rachel to laugh. Sarah was never one to back down from a challenge, she remembered.

"I called ahead and made reservations. You just never know with this place."

Craig let her pass, and then opened the door for her to enter.

As they waited to be seated, she was fully aware of how tall he was, standing behind her. She'd often wondered if her father had been disappointed in her barely-over-five-two stature. Perhaps the fact that she couldn't bounce a ball and catch it again was more worrisome to him. But her little legs could go fast, and the medals, locked away in a box in the basement, proved that.

When the host came back to seat them, Rachel followed, and Craig walked through the restaurant behind her, his hand gently and intimately on her back.

Rachel tucked her lips between her teeth to keep them from chattering. She could do this, she repeated to herself. She could have a meal with the man and say goodbye. Hell, they'd lived twenty miles from one another for ten years and hadn't felt the need to be together. One hour of her life wouldn't change its course, or break any other promises she'd made to her beloved father.

CHAPTER 8

Τ he host sat them in a corner booth with high backs and lots of privacy. Well, Craig thought, if you were going to catch up with an old flame, privately was the way to do that.

He waited for her to hang her coat on the hook on the outside of the booth and climb in before he took off his coat and hung it up. Not that he expected any calls or texts, but he decided to leave his phone in the pocket and give her his undivided attention.

"I don't think I've ever been here," Craig said as he picked up his menu.

"It was one of Dad's favorite places. You know how he loved his chimichangas."

The very mention of it made Craig laugh. "He did like them. Do you come here often then?"

Rachel shook her head. "No, not often." She picked up her menu, looked at it briefly, then set it down.

"You already know what you want?"

"Shrimp cocktail."

Craig smiled and tucked his head back behind his menu. If

she was eating light, she was nervous. Rachel could hold her own when it came to eating, and he knew the small frame only masked that.

He settled on a burrito, and set his menu to the side.

The candle on the table cast a warm glow between them, and if the restaurant was looking for an intimate setting, they'd achieved it.

"How have you been?" Craig finally asked. "Well, before everything happened with your dad," he amended.

"I've been good. My work keeps me busy. I have two dogs that keep me company. I don't live too far from my parents, so you know, family dinner a minimum of once a week."

He did know that. Once upon a time they'd all been part of that family dinner.

"What kind of work do you do?" He hated asking, shouldn't he have known? How did he let her slip from his radar?

"Social work in the public schools. Mostly in high school."

"That doesn't sound easy."

"Kids now days have a lot going on. I don't know that they have more going on than we did. They come to me and ask for help. Of course, you add the internet to the pile, and things do get more tricky but mental wellness is okay to talk about now. They come to me and ask for help."

"So you help people?"

"I try to."

"I'm sure you're good at it. You always did have a good ear."

Wasn't that how it had began? She'd lent him her ear when he needed to vent. She'd been there for him, and all he'd done was break promises and show up ten years later. Guilt had a hefty punch.

"What about you?" she asked, turning the tables. "Still teaching?"

Craig winced. "Yes. I'm teaching community college. Wasn't where I saw myself, but it's a good job."

"You were a high school teacher, right?"

"I was."

"And basketball coach."

He smiled. "Yes. Your dad helped me land that job." He eased back against the booth. "You kept up with me."

"Not much, but when Dad would get information, he passed it on."

He was glad that the server appeared to take their order. That bit of information had hit him harder than he thought it should. The man had been furious with Craig when he'd caught him with his daughter again. But he'd still helped him secure a job—a future. Craig wasn't sure he would have done the same if the roles were switched.

They placed their orders, and when Rachel ordered a margarita, he decided he'd have a beer. Maybe they both needed a little something to take the edge off of the evening.

"Tell me about the other four. How are they?"

So, this was catching up. They could play this game all night. "Alex is in Boston, still. Single. And I think a little lonely. Ray just got divorced, well not just, but it's still fresh. Bruce is currently out of work, and Toby, well Toby is a rich lonely son-of-a-bitch living in some mansion up against the Flatirons. House fit for twenty, and he lives alone."

"He was always so quiet, I never got to know him like I knew the rest of you. But something always told me the wheels in his head were spinning hard."

Craig nodded as their drinks were brought to the table.

He picked up his beer and held it out toward her. She picked up her glass and held it in response.

"To your dad, Coach Diaz, who forever had our backs, no matter what."

He saw the flash of something in her eyes. Sadness? Regret? He wasn't sure.

"To my dad," she said before she took a sip of her drink and set it back down. "The last time I really was caught up on your life was when you got married. Dad showed me all the pictures on Facebook."

Craig winced. "Colleen. Principal at the first school I taught at, five years my senior. She wanted it all. A house, a career, babies."

Rachel picked up her drink and took a long drink until she pushed it away and winced from the brain freeze it gave her.

"You okay?"

"Too much too fast," she said still wincing. "Go on."

"I was just getting my feet wet and I was coaching. Man that was fun," he reminisced. "I was no Coach Diaz, but we were good."

"And babies?" The word shook as she asked it.

"Nah. I wasn't ready for that. I'm not father material. Maybe it stems from not having one around, but it was a sore spot in our relationship. We were married three years and then she left me. I've been single for seven years, and she's been married for five and has two kids. I don't see her but once in a blue moon, and I know she's happy. I was the right guy at the right moment to marry, I guess. Just not the right guy to hold on to."

CHAPTER 9

Rachel took another long drink from her margarita, careful not to get another brain freeze. She couldn't imagine he wasn't worth keeping as a husband. That woman just didn't know him like Rachel had. Then again, she hadn't known the adult Craig Turner, but the young man that he was would have been worthy.

She finished her drink and ordered another.

Craig finished his beer, picked up his water and sipped. "What about you? I don't know anything about you after—" he stopped and took a breath. "After you decided to change schools."

A knot had formed in her belly, and her head now swam with the frozen margarita in her veins. The server set down the second one, and she took a sip.

"Not much to tell. It took me six years to get through school. I found that wanting to be a counselor and having gone through trauma, I had a lot to work through." Her voice had shaken when she said it that way. Did he notice?

"Theo?" Craig asked knowing that his death had caused her great pain.

Rachel nodded, sipping again from her drink. "I hadn't gotten

37

over his death. How could I have?" She knew she didn't have to go on with that. He knew full well she'd been the one to find him.

When she picked up her glass again, her hands shook. There was no doubt Craig noticed, but she was allowed, she told herself. She'd just buried her father, and now a conversation with an old lover was bringing up memories she just didn't want to deal with.

She'd come to the table wanting to catch up, and had all intentions to then just walk away. But the more she drank down the frozen concoction and let it numb her, the less courage she found she actually had.

The server delivered their meals, and it was an opportune time to change conversations away from her. She couldn't be good company with her head swimming the way it was. Rachel didn't usually drink, so this was uncharacteristic.

"You said Sarah kicked your asses in that game." Rachel started a new conversation. "How is she?"

"Tough as nails," Craig said on a laugh as he lifted a bite of his burrito to his mouth. "She can talk the talk and walk the walk. No one intimidates her, and she's still got more skill than any of us."

"And Bruce, is he still googly-eyed over her?"

Craig laughed again. "I don't suppose he'll ever get over her. I don't know if it's just a childhood crush he hangs on to or if it's that Alex forbids anything between them." He took another bite. "But we know how that usually works out."

The words had rolled off his tongue, but Rachel was sure he didn't think it through. Her father had forbade them from seeing each other, and it had only made them lie to the man they both cherished.

Maybe he'd mostly forgotten about it—about them.

. . .

38

THE CONVERSATION BOUNCED around from the past to the present and was filled with memories of Rachel's father and the kind man that he was.

She'd been unable to finish her meal, and the margaritas still swam in her head. When the bill arrived, she made a move for it. Here she'd invited the man to dinner so she could clear her conscience, instead, she'd gotten drunk.

Craig grabbed the ticket first. "This is my treat. You have no idea how much I needed this. And all I can hope is that it was as nice for you. I'm actually honored that you asked me to meet you. I'm sure your mother could use your company."

"She's had it, and currently it's not good company."

"It was good for me," he said pulling out his wallet and handing the server his credit card. "We should do this again."

That shouldn't have brought her to tears, but it had. Maybe it was the alcohol, or the moment, she didn't know.

Craig slid out of the booth and a moment later moved in next to her, wrapping his arm around her shoulders. Instinctively, she rested her head against him.

"Oh, sweetheart, I didn't mean to upset you," he said as he ran his hand over her hair and then pressed a kiss to the top of her head.

"I'm sorry. Maybe I should have waited a few weeks to see you. This isn't fair to you. Not after all these years."

Craig placed his finger under her chin and lifted her face so that their eyes met. "Life got in our way, Rach. I've been there for your losses and your wins. I'm always going to be there. Maybe this is a new start for our friendship."

Rachel pursed her lips to keep them from trembling. "Thank you."

"I also think I should give you a ride home."

She shook her head. "You can't do that. Tomorrow is Monday. We both have work."

"We'll figure it out. Or we can call your brother, or get you an Uber."

No. She'd started this night needing to be with him, and if he was going to offer to take her home, she'd take him up on it. It would mean that at some point they'd probably have to meet back up, and maybe by then she'd have some courage to talk to him.

"I'll take you up on it, if you're okay with that."

"Wouldn't have offered, otherwise," he said brushing his hand over her hair again.

The server returned with his card, and Craig slid out of the booth and stood up.

"My first class tomorrow isn't until eleven," he said taking her coat off the hook and holding it out for her.

Rachel slid from the booth and put her arms into the coat.

"Thank you." She buttoned it up as he put on his own coat. "I have to be at work at seven. I'll have Hal come get me and take me to work."

Craig pulled on his gloves. "How about I pick you up after work to come get your car, and maybe we could have dinner again?"

Rachel swallowed the lump in her throat. "That's out of your way."

"I'd really like to. I only have two classes on Mondays."

She gave it a moment's thought. "Okay. I'd like that."

CHAPTER 10

The moment Hal pulled up in front of her house, Rachel opened the front door. She gave each of the dogs a kiss and a pat on the head, before shutting the door and hurrying to the car, her bags slipping from her shoulders.

She pulled open the car door and slid into the warm seat her brother had preheated for her. "Thank you," she said. "I owe you."

"I have a list, and it never gets any smaller," he teased as he pulled away from her house. "And where is your car?"

Rachel turned her head and looked at him through her dark sunglasses. The sun wasn't bright enough to warrant them, but two margaritas had hung her over, and any light hurt.

"It's at *Juanita's*," she said, and he nodded slowly.

"Margaritas?"

"Yes. Don't judge me."

"No judgement. So who brought you home?"

Rachel held her bags to her tightly. "Craig Turner."

Her brother's head nodded slowly, but he refrained from saying anything more, though she was sure he had plenty to say.

"I have a ride after work to pick it up. So you're off the hook there," she said lightly, hoping to diffuse the mood as much as possible.

"Craig Turner?" he asked, and she winced.

"Yes."

"He's off limits, Rach."

"I'm nearly thirty and Dad is gone."

"And you're going to rush right back to him? What the hell is this?"

Rachel pulled off the dark glasses. "Who are you to care?"

"You're going to go there? Are you kidding me?"

She slid back on the glasses and eased back in the seat. "No. Just don't worry about me."

"Right."

"He's a nice guy."

"I know that. Dad knew that. Everyone knows that."

"Then don't worry."

Hal shook his head, but she knew he wouldn't say anything else. He had all the reason in the world to worry about her getting involved with Craig, but that wasn't what was happening. They were going to have a few meals, that was all—or so she tried to convince herself.

It was during Craig's second class, in the middle of a riveting lecture on the Civil War, that he received the text from Rachel with the address to her school.

I'll be done at 3:30, she added.

He took a moment to reply. *I'll be there.*

Luckily the lecture was nearly over, and the class was due to take a test. That gave Craig a few moments to collect himself.

He was going to have dinner with Rachel Diaz for the second night in a row. Sure, it was circumstantial, but what else would it mean? Were they going to draw on their friendship, or was there something left from what they'd had a decade ago?

No, he tried to clear his mind of that. That was off limits.

AT THREE-THIRTY HE pulled up in front of the high school and parked in the parking lot. As a teacher, the vibe of teenagers in cars and milling around shouldn't give him anxiety, but he found that it did. Had he removed himself that far from the true educational field?

Community college, though it had its share of nineteen-year-olds, was completely different. Those in community college seemed to be there because they were ready to learn, and most of them were footing the bill themselves. There was a different maturity level all together. Could he go back to teaching the youth of America?

A crowd of girls walked out the front of the school, and side by side with them was Rachel. Was it possible she looked as if she belonged? She had nearly fifteen years on the girls who giggled around her, but she fit in. Just as he'd remembered her.

As the girls went one way, they waved at her and he could see the connection she had with the students. They trusted her. Had all of those girls told her their secrets?

He watched as she scanned the parking lot looking for his car, and she smiled when she saw it.

Craig opened the door and stepped outside. He hurried to the other side of the car and opened the door.

Rachel grinned up at him. "You always were a gentleman."

"Remember, my grandmother made me take those classes."

She laughed easily. "I do remember you mentioning it."

Rachel slid into the car and Craig closed the door before walking back around and climbing in the other side.

Craig pulled out of the parking space and headed toward the

exit. "I guess it's a little too early for dinner. We could go get your car and take it back to your house."

He caught the worry that flashed across her face and then disappeared. Maybe that had sounded too forward. After all, they were starting new with the communication and the friendship.

"We could do that. I have to go home and let the dogs out for a little bit."

"Right. You have two?"

She smiled wide. "Rover is my tea-cup poodle and Clyde is my golden retriever."

That warranted him turning his head to study her, and seeing that she was humored.

"And the big dog doesn't step on the little one?"

"It happens, but he's very protective of her."

"Her? The poodle is a she and her name is Rover?"

That made her laugh and ease against the seat. "I rescued her. The name came with her and it was just too cute to change. And out of the two she's the more ferocious."

"Sounds like her owner. Small package, has a loud bark."

Rachel appeared appalled, but the smile still settled on her lips. "I always could hold my own."

"Oh yes you could. I always figured that was because you were brought up with horny, annoying teenagers in your house. I'm sure that on more than one occasion you had to stand up for yourself."

The smile faded and she worried her lip. "I think because of my bark, I didn't have to do that too often at all. In the years that Dad had his teams around, you seem to be the only one that ever caught me."

Just the acknowledgment of it punched him in the gut. Yes, he had caught her, and then they'd been caught.

CHAPTER 11

C raig followed her home from the restaurant and parked on the street when she pulled her car into the garage. Rachel gathered her bags as he walked toward her.

"You are close to your parents' house, aren't you?" he asked looking at her house and then at the surrounding neighborhood.

"I like the area."

"What's not to like? I can wait for you in the car," he offered.

"No. You don't have to do that. Come in for a moment. Meet the dogs. They'll let me know what they think of you."

"I'm never a good first impression," Craig said as she passed by him, but that warranted a glance back in his direction. He had no idea how good his first impression was.

He didn't look as formal today. The jacket he wore looked like every other puffer jacket in Boulder. He was dressed in a casual shirt, a pair of jeans, and she supposed comfortable shoes since he stood on his feet all day.

Rachel walked to the front door, the keys in her hand, and she unlocked the locks.

Carefully she pushed open the door, knowing full well Rover would be at her feet the moment she stepped in.

Without fail, the tiny dog appeared from around the coat stand and barked her welcome.

"There's my girl." She reached down and petted the top of her head as she hung her bags on the rack.

Once her hands were free, she bent down to pick the little dog up, moving so that Craig could walk into the house.

He stepped in and closed the door behind him.

"This is the mighty Miss Rover," Rachel held the dog in the crook of her arm, and Craig cautiously reached his hand toward Rover's head and scratched behind her ears.

Rachel watched the interaction carefully. Rover didn't care for anyone who came into their house, except her parents and Hal.

"I think she likes you," she said, smiling up at Craig.

"What's not to like?" he teased, and she had to agree.

Rachel watched as Clyde rounded the corner and brushed up against Craig. He jumped at first, but Clyde wasn't fazed.

"I didn't see him come up," he said, kneeling down to be on Clyde's level so they were eye to eye as Clyde sniffed his hands and then allowed him to rub his head.

"For being a big dog, he's silent. And he seems to like you too."

"Did I pass the first test?"

"Test?"

"The dogs like me, so I must be okay?"

Rachel set Rover on the floor and she took off and Clyde followed. "What's not to like, right?" she mimicked his phrase as Craig stood, and she watched him rise to tower over her. "I need to feed them and let them out. Then I'll be ready to go. C'mon back."

CRAIG FOLLOWED Rachel down the hallway past her small living room, with the large TV, to the tiny kitchen off the back of the house.

She pushed open the back door, and the two dogs bounded

46

through the yard. Clyde chased Rover, overshooting her position and running back to nudge his nose under her.

"Rover is in charge, isn't she?"

"Absolutely," Rachel confirmed as she picked up the food bowls and set them on the small kitchen table.

Craig watched as she opened the pantry and scooped their food out of a sealed container and filled the bowls before setting them back on the floor.

"We can order in, if you've been gone from them all day," Craig offered and she lifted her eyes to meet his.

"Really?"

"Listen, I don't care where we eat, I was just excited to get to see you one more time."

Her eyes went wide. "You were?"

Craig tucked his hands into the pockets of his coat. "Is that okay?"

"Of course," she said as she moved back to the pantry. "I wasn't sure how you were going to react to me when I texted you after the funeral."

"I wasn't sure what kind of reception I was going to get at the funeral from your family. Your dad might have set me on the right path, and helped me land my first job, but..."

A flush crossed her cheeks. "I know. No need to go into detail there."

"Right." He rocked back on his heels. "I guess what we need to do is establish some things."

Rachel rested her hands on the back of one of the chairs at the table. "What kind of things?"

"We're adults."

"Obviously."

"We should be able to handle what happened between us a decade ago and be friends, like before."

"Absolutely."

"We're not hurting anyone or endangering our future," he said using the Coach's words.

Rachel winced. "Right."

"And, I've missed you."

Her lips curled up into a smile. "You have?"

"Yeah. Does that surprise you?"

She nodded. "Yes."

"Why?"

"Because after you graduated, I didn't see you after that summer."

Craig raked his fingers through his hair and crossed his arms. "Yeah, my dad messed me up that summer. He got into my head." He cringed when he thought of it. "Then I went on to get that job your dad vouched for me on, and you left the state to go to school."

Rachel turned her back to him, opened the cupboard and pulled down two wine glasses. "Last minute decision."

"You had track scholarships."

She opened her refrigerator and pulled out a bottle of wine. "Let's order dinner. We have a lot of time to catch up."

He wasn't sure what had made her so nervous, but she was pouring him a glass of wine, and inviting him to stay in her house. It was a start, he figured. They could work on the friendship aspect over dinner, with her pups at their feet.

Rachel handed him a glass of wine, and held the other in her hand. "I feel like we need another toast."

"Okay. What are we toasting?"

"To old friendships?"

Craig tapped his glass to hers.

CHAPTER 12

I n keeping with a friendly and casual dinner, Rachel ordered pizza from the small family-owned restaurant on the next block. They decided to take the dogs for a walk to pick up their order. Craig laughed as Rachel handed him Clyde's leash as she tucked Rover into her coat and zipped it up so that only her tiny nose could be seen.

"You could make her a saddle and let her ride Clyde," he teased as they began their trek toward the restaurant.

"You think I haven't thought about that?"

Craig took in the neighborhood as they walked down the street. "This is a nice area."

"Old, but nice."

"Old holds its own. The neighborhood I live in has had its transformations. I remember my great grandparents living there, and then it got run down when we were teenagers. Now, it's a hot spot with restaurants, professionals, families, and coffee shops."

"Where do you live?" she asked.

"Highland, or as my parents would rather, North Denver."

That made her chuckle. "My aunt and uncle feel the same. If

you slap some paint on the buildings and give it a new name, it gets new life but undermines the people who established the area."

Yeah, they understood each other, he thought.

Clyde wandered up onto the grass of another house, and Craig steered him back. "What would you have been doing tonight if we hadn't made these plans?"

"I don't think these are the plans we made," she said nudging him. "I had some food that a neighbor brought over when Dad died. In fact, I had so much food brought to me, I had to freeze some of it."

"It's nice to know people still do that."

"They did it when he was sick too. There is decency in the world."

Guilt twisted in his gut. He should have been one of those people who reached out when Coach was sick. He should have called, texted, or dropped by with food too. But he'd gone on with his life as normal. It was selfish, he told himself. Hadn't they all rallied around Coach and his family when Theo died? Shouldn't they have done that for them when Coach got sick too?

"I should have visited him when he was sick," Craig said, and Rachel turned to look at him. He averted his gaze so she wouldn't see that his eyes had gone damp.

"He would have liked that, but he wasn't always up for visitors. Once he was in the thick of it, he slept a lot." She reached for his hand and gave it a squeeze. "So, don't beat yourself up over it."

The gesture was so intimate, he had to feel it out by interlacing their fingers and holding on. Rachel didn't pull away.

THERE WAS A WARMTH BETWEEN THEM, even as the sun began to dip down over the mountains and the air cooled. Rachel absorbed the intimacy of his hand in hers.

This hadn't been what she'd expected when she'd texted him

after her father's funeral, but it might have been just what she needed—what they both needed. She understood he was in mourning too, and just like all mourning, guilt mixed with it.

Was it possible to mourn without feeling guilt, she wondered? Even trained in her field, she wasn't sure she could answer that. It seemed to her that guilt was attached to every emotion.

Rover shifted in her jacket, and she had to drop her hand from Craig's to keep the small dog in place.

"I want to say she's a spoiled dog, but maybe she's just lucky," Craig teased.

"Oh, she's spoiled. They both are. But, they spoil me," she admitted as she pressed a kiss to the top of Rover's head.

They came to the corner and pushed the button for the walk signal.

"Do you have room for her in your coat?" Rachel asked as they crossed the street.

"I can go in and get the pizza."

She shook her head. "No, because if you go in, you'll pay for it. This is my treat," she said as she took the small dog out of her coat and handed her to Craig.

Craig tucked the tiny dog into his coat outside of the restaurant and zipped her in comfortably.

"I'll be right back."

Rachel walked inside and approached the counter. She gave them her name and looked out the window as they put the order together.

She watched as Craig crouched down in front of Clyde, who stuck his nose into Craig's jacket to check on his friend.

It was sweet and considerate of him, she thought. He took the dogs seriously, and she knew it wasn't an act to get her attention. That was who Craig Turner was.

Rachel let out a steady breath. Ten years ago, she'd banked on that considerate soul. She'd given herself to Craig, but her expectations had been too high. She'd been too young to understand the ways of the world. Every day she watched the students she worked with go through the same emotions she'd had when she was their age. It had all seemed so final. Time was of the essence, and there was no patience for years to pass and for them to grow into adults. It was all or nothing—or so she thought back then.

Rachel sucked in a hard breath. She felt the panic attack coming on, and it was being created by her own mind.

Breathe in. Breathe out, she reminded herself. The past was the past, and she no longer dealt with things the way she had back then. She was almost thirty, and trained in knowing when the mind was playing tricks on her. What she went through ten years ago wasn't going to happen again, even if she never saw Craig Turner again.

Rachel looked out the window again, and watched as he ran his hand over Clyde's head and scratched behind his ears.

One minute at a time, Rach. One minute at a time.

CHAPTER 13

R achel stepped out into the cold, the warm pizza in her hand.

"Smells good," Craig said as he stood, careful to hold his jacket to protect the dog nuzzled up against him.

"Do you want me to take her?" Rachel asked.

"I got it. You carry the pizza."

Side by side they walked back up the street. Craig held the front of his coat with Rover inside, and Clyde walked beside him as if he'd been trained to do it.

"How did you win over my dogs?" she asked, hoping the tone of her comment was more teasing than accusing.

"Honey, I win everyone over," he replied with a laugh. "Actually, I don't know. We had a talk while you were inside. We established some rules about sharing your time. They seem to be okay with it."

"Sharing my time? Does that mean we'll be seeing you again?" she asked as they came to the crosswalk and she pushed the button for the walk light.

Craig looked down at her and she caught the glance. "I'd like to see you more."

Because his words set off little sparks inside of her, she had to struggle to keep the smile that formed on her lips small, when in actuality it wanted to grow wide.

The light signaled for them to walk, and they crossed the street in silence and remained that way until they walked up the front step of Rachel's house.

"Hold this while I open the door," she said, handing him the pizza and pulling her keys out of her pocket.

RACHEL UNLOCKED the door and pushed it open. Clyde pranced straight inside, his leash dragging on the ground, as if it were his job to check out the house before they stepped in. Rachel followed, taking the pizza from Craig.

Craig stepped into the house, and Rover's nose immediately poked out of the top of his jacket. "You're ready to run and play too, aren't you?" he asked as he unzipped his jacket and pulled the tiny dog out, setting her on the floor. She took off through the house, looking for her brother, who came back to have his leash removed.

Clyde looked up at Rachel, who still held the pizza, then turned his attention to Craig. With a chuckle, Craig knelt down and unhooked the leash from his collar before Clyde took off after Rover.

"They don't like everyone that walks into this house," Rachel said as she handed him the pizza so she could take off her coat and hang it up. "Do you have treats in your pocket?"

"I'm telling you, I'm likable."

Rachel hung her coat up on the rack, and took the pizza from Craig. "I agree," she said as she walked back toward the kitchen, turning on lights in the living room as she walked through.

Craig took an extra moment to collect himself. What was he doing? He'd promised Coach to never get involved with his daughter again, and here he was.

It was innocent, he thought as he unzipped his jacket and shrugged it off. But how long could it remain innocent if he pursued this friendship, he wondered as he hung up his coat.

He was a grown man, he reminded himself. Rachel was a woman, not an eighteen-year-old. They both had more at stake than a broken heart. But they also were mature enough to handle a relationship, should this friendship thing work out in their favor.

"Are you coming in?" Rachel's voice came from the back of the house.

"Just hanging up my coat," he said back.

Rover and Clyde were sitting next to each other, their size difference humorous to the onlooker. They patiently waited for Rachel to attend to them.

Craig watched as Rachel scooped peanut butter out of a container and spread it onto two small plates. She set them on the floor by their food bowls and the two dogs scurried toward the plates.

She returned to the container and twisted the lid back on.

Craig leaned up against the wall and watched her. "You're a good dog mom," he complimented.

Rachel laughed as she put the peanut butter back in the cupboard. "They've kept me sane. I think I have a bag of salad in the refrigerator if you need something other than pizza."

"Just pizza is fine for me." He stood and walked toward her, as she pulled down two more plates for them.

"Beer, soda, or water?"

"I'll take a beer."

Rachel set down the plates, opened the refrigerator, and pulled out two bottles of beer. She handed them to Craig to open.

"We can eat out in the living room and turn on the TV," she suggested.

He wondered if that was to keep it more casual, and if they

turned on the TV, they wouldn't have time to talk. Or maybe, she was just being relaxed around him.

Rachel dished two pieces of pizza onto each plate and then closed the box. As she turned, she handed Craig his plate, their fingers brushing, and he handed her a beer.

He couldn't help but take another moment to look at her. She was just as he'd always remembered her. Those dark searing eyes, that beautiful silky hair, and a fit body that made him long to hold her.

"What?" she asked and he realized just by his proximity, he'd cornered her in the kitchen.

"Sorry, I was just looking at you. I've thought of you a lot over the years, and you haven't changed a bit."

A flush filled her cheeks. "You've thought of me?"

"A lot."

"I don't know what to do with that information."

Craig smiled. "You've always been important to me."

"I haven't talked to you in ten years."

"We had lives to live and careers to build."

"And a promise to my father," she reminded him.

"And a promise to your father," he repeated and took a step back so that she could pass by him.

He followed her to the living room where she set her plate and beer on the coffee table. As she searched for the remote to the TV, he watched her again.

"Are you comfortable with me here? I'm wondering if I should go," he said and watched as her eyes lifted to look at him.

"I don't want you to go."

"I just figured I'd better ask."

They stood staring at each other for a moment before she moved to him and took his plate and beer, setting them down next to hers.

"My dad isn't here, Craig. I shouldn't even have brought that up."

"It's in the back of our minds," he admitted. "If we're just feeling out an old friendship over pizza, then it shouldn't matter, right?"

Rachel stepped closer to him. "It shouldn't matter because we're adults. We should be able to feel out friendships, or whatever it is."

"And what is it?" he heard his voice grow deeper as she took another step toward him.

Rachel licked her lips as she placed her hands on his chest and looked up at him. "I don't know, but I'd like to find out," she said on a breath as she lifted on her toes, wrapped her arms around his neck, and pulled him down to meet her mouth with his.

CHAPTER 14

C raig pulled her in, their mouths feverishly working against the other's. When her tongue pressed against his, his hands gripped her waist and held her tighter as his knees grew weak.

He'd been here a million times—only in his mind.

Why was it that this woman had always had a hold on him? He'd watched her grow into a woman, fell in love with her when she'd become an adult, and the feeling had never left him.

Craig let his hand slide from her waist, and over her bottom. He absorbed the moan that came from her, and it shook through him.

With her arms wrapped around his neck, he hoisted her to his hips, and her legs came around him.

The kiss deepened, and their breath came faster. They'd created heat like this before.

Craig carried Rachel to the couch and laid her down beneath him. Her legs still circled him and their lips never parted.

What had they started, he wondered as he trailed his lips from hers and down her slender neck. Was this what they'd waited all these years for? Would they handle what was coming better than they'd handled it when they were younger?

Rachel tugged at the hem of his shirt, untucking it from his pants. When it was free, he felt her hands on his skin. There was no stopping the momentum between them now. This fire had obviously never burnt out. And no promise would stop them from continuing what they'd started so many years ago.

RACHEL REACHED for the buttons on the front of his shirt that she'd untucked from his pants, but her fingers weren't nimble enough to free him from the fabric while her breath was taken by his kisses.

She felt him, pressed against her. Had he dreamt of this as often as she had? Had she been constantly on his mind, as he had been on hers?

Should she feel guilt because she was breaking a promise to her father? If she was, it hadn't surfaced yet. Then again, she'd wanted this for so long, she knew she couldn't stop it.

Craig buried his face into the crevice of her neck and she pressed her hands to his bare chest as he moved against her. Every womanly urge stirred in her. In the back of her head she knew there was a chance that this was for the moment. They'd end up in bed together, and maybe have a meal again, but it might end. Then again, it might just be the start of something—the continuation of what long ago should have been.

Craig moved his mouth back to hers as he slipped his hands under her shirt and her gasp pulled her from him. His eyes opened to watch her, but she knew she hadn't panicked him when his eyes went dark and his mouth moved back to hers.

As his hands moved under her shirt to cup her breasts, the doorbell rang, followed by knocking on the door.

Craig eased back and Rachel let out a growl as the dogs scurried to the door, barking.

"I'm going to kill whoever that is," she cursed as Craig rocked back and climbed off of her as she swung her feet to the floor.

Rachel walked toward the door, hushing the dogs, as she straightened her shirt and noticed that Craig did the same.

She picked up Rover, and held her to her chest, as she nudged Clyde back. Rachel looked through the hole in the door and shook her head. "Seriously?"

Rachel pulled open the door and her brother stepped inside. "God it's freezing out here. You have company? There's a car..." he stopped as he saw Craig standing in the living room. "You do have company."

Hal walked toward Craig, extending his hand.

"It's nice to see you, Hal."

"I forgot you were going to pick her up and take her to her car. Plans changed?" Hal asked as he turned back to his sister.

"We decided to get some pizza. Would you like to stay?"

Hal shifted a glance between them. "Ya know, I think I would like to stay."

Of course he would, she thought. She'd seen his eyes when he'd noticed Craig standing there. Luckily, Craig had managed to put himself back together. But there was no doubt in her mind that he knew exactly what they'd been up to.

Rachel started toward the kitchen and Hal followed. From the corner of her eye, she watched Craig pick up his plate and beer, and sit in the chair, not on the couch next to where she would be sitting.

Hal knelt down and picked up Rover, who had begun to climb up his leg. As soon as he held the pup to his chest, Clyde moved in mimicking Rover's previous actions.

"You think that I'm going to pick you up too?" he asked Clyde, as he scrubbed his hand over the dog's head. "You have no idea the two of you aren't the same size," he teased as Rachel put two slices of pizza on the plate she'd taken down for him.

"Do you want a beer too?"

She watched as he glanced toward Craig and back to her. "Sure. Do you have a craft one in there?"

"I have the ones you brought when you were here last."

"That'll work." He set Rover down next to Clyde and took the plate from Rachel.

She bent into the refrigerator, and nearly screamed when she came back up and Hal was face to face with her.

"What are you two really doing?" he whispered.

"We're eating cold pizza, just like you are," she bit back and shut the door.

Hal let out a hum, but she knew he wasn't done with the inquisition. There would be no getting rid of him tonight. He would stay as long as he had to, to get the answers he was looking for.

Rachel just wasn't sure she had any for him. They might have been headed for something monumental, but now she would never know.

CHAPTER 15

Craig sat back in the comfy chair and sipped the beer that Rachel had given him. He wasn't sure if Hal had been a curse or a savior to their situation. The teenager in him was disappointed. The adult thought it was better to have disengaged. But the adult wasn't sure he was right.

"So you're a teacher?" Hal asked Craig as he sat down with his plate of pizza and beer.

"I am. Who would have thought?"

"I remember you struggling in school."

"I did. I like to think it makes me a sympathetic teacher. I've been in their shoes."

Hal nodded. "You're not coaching?"

Craig shook his head. "It's been a few years. The teams I had did well. Maybe someday I'll get back into it." Craig picked up a slice of pizza and took a bite. "You're still military?" he asked Hal who nodded slowly.

"On leave for a bit to help Mom get situated."

Rachel plopped down next to her brother on the couch. "Mom will be fine. I think she's tired of us hovering over her."

Hal shook his head. "It's still fresh. He hasn't been gone an entire week yet. You just don't let go of the caretaker role and not give a shit anymore."

"I don't think that's what I was saying," Rachel bit back. "I just mean, she'd probably like us to stop hovering."

Craig watched the exchange and wondered how normal it was for them to argue as they were. Hal always had Rachel's back, but sometimes he'd cross the line between sibling and guardian. And hadn't he been on the receiving end of Hal's anger more than once? He knew that his evening wasn't going to pick up where it had left off.

Craig finished his beer and mindfully ate his slices of pizza, sure not to choke from eating so quickly. For everyone's sake, he needed to make his exit.

As he set down his plate, Clyde sauntered over and rested his head on Craig's lap. He ran his hand over the dog's head.

"He likes you," Rachel said. "I told you, they don't like anyone."

Hal let out a grunt. "She's right. They don't like anyone."

"Well, then, that makes me happy." He shifted a glance toward Rachel whose lips had turned upward in a strained grin. "I should be heading out. I have exams to grade," he said as he maneuvered out of the chair, moving the dog.

Craig picked up his trash and walked back to the kitchen. Rachel followed.

"I'm sorry," she said softly. "He's being a total ass."

"And he deserves to be. No one is going to accept me in your life, and I get that."

"They'll have to get used to it," she said stepping in closer to him. "I'd like you back in my life."

Craig sucked in a breath. Was he ready for that? Then again, what did he have to lose?

Rachel lifted to her toes and pressed a quick kiss to his lips. "Come back on Friday. I'd like to cook for you."

"Are you sure?"

"I invited you, didn't I?"

"I'd like that."

Craig reached for her hand, gave it a squeeze, and then walked back to the living room. "It's been nice to catch up. I'd love to do more of that," he said to Hal, who stood to shake his hand.

"Be safe getting home. There's lots of drunks on ninety-three and thirty-six," he rattled off the two main highways that would get Craig out of town.

"I'll be careful."

Rachel followed him to the door where he shrugged on his coat and pulled his keys from his pockets.

"I'll see you on Friday."

Rachel locked eyes with him. "Bring an overnight bag."

RACHEL CLOSED the door and walked back to the living room where her ass of a brother sat on the couch eating his pizza. She picked up her plate and beer, and occupied the chair that Craig had just vacated.

"Super nice how you were able to push my company out the door," she smirked as she lifted her cold pizza to her lips and took a bite.

"You don't need any complications right now."

"Screw you. I'd like some complications. You don't have control over me anymore. I'm not a child."

"Fine. Then go and find someone who didn't cause you drama."

"He didn't."

"Really? Not only did he, but so did his family. Do we need to dive into that?" Hal asked as his voice rose and he set down his plate.

"Ten years, Hal. Ten. I'm not who I was then and neither is he. I don't expect the perfect fairy-tale. I don't expect anything."

"Good, because I'm damn sure that's what you'll get —nothing."

Rachel set her plate on the coffee table. "I don't get why everyone is against Craig."

"No one is against Craig. Everyone likes him just fine. It's the two of you we're against."

"Why?"

"Lift your sleeves."

Rachel bit down hard enough her jaw ached. She picked up her plate, kicked her feet up on the table, and bit into the pizza again, only this time she continued to eat until the slice was gone.

Craig was not completely to blame for the depressive state she fell into when he graduated and moved on. Though, his father's interactions with her family, and Craig's attitude change when his father appeared for the first time in his life, hadn't helped. But her trauma wasn't his fault. Years later, hours of therapy, and career training had proven that to her.

Her genetic makeup hadn't done her any favors either. Depression ran through her veins as thick as the blood. Theo'd been affected by it too.

She understood Hal's concern, but she also knew how she felt when she looked into Craig Turner's eyes. She'd like to think that she could appreciate him and walk away, but deep down inside of her he stirred feelings she'd never lost. She loved the man. Oh, she might have fallen in love with him as a teenager, but those feelings had never gone away. Having him wrap his arms around her and kiss her, it had only reignited the flame. And she'd be damned if a promise to her father, or a mistake in her past, kept her from him. Rachel was still in love with Craig, and she was being given a second chance.

CHAPTER 16

As Craig's class settled into the room, he received a group text from Alex that he'd safely returned to Boston. He took a moment to thank each of them for their contribution to his weekend, saying *my brothers, you have no idea how much I needed that and how much it meant to me*. When Alex added a jab at Bruce, warning him to stay away from his sister in his absence, it warranted a chuckle from Craig, which caught the attention of a few students.

After classes, exam grading, class planning, and a staff meeting, Craig was finally on his way home. There was solace in having a job that had him home before the traffic grew heavy most days.

When Craig pulled up in front of his one-hundred-year-old, brick, bungalow style home, he noticed the car parked on the street out front. He pulled up into his driveway, and to the back of the house to park his car in the detached garage. Before he even climbed out of his car, Bruce walked up the driveway.

"Hey, pal. What are you doing here?" Craig asked as he pulled his messenger bag from the backseat.

Bruce tucked his hands into the pockets of his coat. "Let's just call it boredom."

Craig laughed as he pushed the button to close the garage door. "Ah, you're bored and you thought of me. Flattered?" Craig let out a hum. "I'm just not sure."

That warranted a chuckle from Bruce. "There's a Nuggets game on early tonight. Thought we could have a beer or two, order a pizza, I don't know."

Craig hiked the bag up on his shoulder. This was one of his chosen brothers, who obviously needed an ear. Well, wasn't that what they'd all needed lately, and hadn't that been the reason he'd accepted Rachel's invitation for dinner on Sunday, and again on Monday? Perhaps that's what he told himself to ward off the guilt of knowing he was going to break a promise just to see her again.

CRAIG AND BRUCE walked through the back door of the house. Craig hung his bag by the door, pulled his coat off, and hung it over the bag. Bruce hung his coat on the rack, and followed Craig into the kitchen.

"I have light beer, and a few craft beers," Craig offered as he pulled open the door to the refrigerator.

"Light is fine," Bruce said as he cocked his head to look into the refrigerator. "A few craft beers? There are two shelves of beer in your fridge," he laughed.

"My mom sent me a membership to a craft beer club, and so did my sister." He pulled out two beers, closed the door with his hip, and walked to the counter to pop the tops off the bottles using an opener mounted by the sink. The caps fell off into a cup.

Bruce took the bottle that was handed to him. "Thanks."

Craig took his first sip. "You doing okay?"

Bruce shrugged. "Long day. Unproductive. Okay," he let out a breath, "a straight up crappy day."

"What happened?"

68

"Three interviews. Three rejections. I have a pimple on my ass, and my electric bill was double this month because I've been home all month."

Craig lifted his bottle to his lips to keep the smile from surfacing. It was true friends that would throw in a personal problem in the middle of all the other problems as if it were as big a deal as being unemployed with bills.

"That's rough. I don't work in a place where I can even offer you a job," he said, thinking he was in an industry where you had to be certified and overly educated to get a damn job. "I have no idea what to do about the pimple on your ass, but I can loan you some money if you need some to carry you."

Now Bruce laughed before his eyes darkened with worry and sadness. "I would never want to do that," he said. "But I really appreciate the offer. I think I need to downsize."

Craig leaned against the counter. "Have you considered asking Toby for a job?"

Bruce nodded as he sipped his beer. "Last resort. I should downsize. I'm paying rent on a house, and I don't even spend time in all of it. I'm pathetic. I eat over the sink and watch TV from my bed. Why have a whole house?"

Craig chewed his bottom lip and then drank down his beer. Opening the door on the cupboard, under the sink, he discarded the empty bottle into his recycling.

"C'mon," he said. "I want to show you something."

Craig walked to the back door and turned to go down the stairs that led to the basement. Bruce followed, and when they hit the bottom step, Craig flipped the switch to turn on the light.

For the past six years, remodeling the basement had been Craig's pastime. It occupied his mind when he switched jobs, and gave him some purpose. Now he knew why he'd done it.

In the main room, he'd created an entertainment area, complete with a pool table, dart board, sofa, and a TV mounted on the wall.

Bruce whistled when he stepped into the room. "This is nice."

"I'm happy with how it turned out." He turned to the next room and turned on the light. "This was a son-of-a-bitch," he offered as Bruce looked over his shoulder into the bathroom.

"Did you put that in yourself?"

"Yep. Built the walls, added the shower, toilet, and sink. Learned how to tile in this room."

"You did a hell of a job."

"Thanks." Craig turned off the light and walked to the next room. "There are two bedrooms upstairs, but I figured this could be a guest room and the other upstairs could be an office."

Bruce looked around the room, walking in and pulling the Murphy bed down. "Nice use of space."

"That's what I thought. So what do you think?"

"What do I think? I think you did a great job."

"Would you be interested in renting it?"

Bruce pushed the bed back into place and turned toward Craig, his brows drawn together. "This room?"

"The whole basement actually. You can use the kitchen too. I was just thinking maybe it would be helpful to you. And teachers don't make bank, so it would help me too."

Bruce chewed his bottom lip, crossing his arms in front of him. "I don't want to burden any of my friends."

"No burden. I can't think of anyone I'd rather have in my home."

Bruce looked around the small room and a smile curled on his lips. "You are a true friend, my brother," he said holding his hand out to Craig. "I'd be honored to live here."

Craig shook his hand. Though he missed Coach Diaz, he was grateful that even in the end, his passing had brought his boys back together, and now it appeared they were going to keep that relationship intact.

CHAPTER 17

Aside from a few text messages, Craig hadn't talked to Rachel all week. She'd never really mentioned a time for dinner, but he thought if he arrived by six on Friday night, he could help cook, or maybe he'd be right on time.

Nerves had rattled him again as he pulled up in front of her house. In the back seat, he had a duffle bag with a change of clothes and his toothbrush. Wasn't that what she'd said to bring? He'd leave it in the car, just in case he misunderstood her motive or changed her mind.

As he stepped out into the street and grabbed the bottle of wine he'd brought from the other seat, he saw her standing in the doorway. She was dressed casually in a tank top and yoga pants, her hair piled atop her head. Now he wondered if he'd misread the invite.

"You're just in time," she called toward him as she pulled a baggy, long sleeved top over her, hiding the curves he'd been appreciating. "I just put dinner in the oven. There's a salad that needs tossing."

Craig gave the car door a nudge with his hip to close, and

started toward the house. "I thought you were going to make me do some yoga."

She laughed easily. "I already did that. You're off the hook."

Rachel smiled as he neared the door. There was comfort between them, and the fact that she hadn't fussed over herself for him proved that. And that was what he'd always loved about Rachel Diaz.

Craig handed her the bottle in his hand as he approached. "I didn't know what I was pairing with, so I brought a red."

"It'll pair just fine," she said taking the bottle from him. "Where's your overnight bag?" Her brows rose as she asked.

"I didn't want to be presumptuous."

"There's no presumptions. I told you I wanted you to stay."

Craig stepped through the door and immediately wrapped an arm around her waist, pulling her close, and smoothing his other hand into her hair. "Are you sure that's what you want?"

"From as far back as I can remember," she said, rising on her toes and pressing her lips to his. "I don't want to scare you off." Her voice softened.

Craig drew in a breath. "I'm not scared," he admitted as he hoisted her to his hips and she wrapped her legs around him. Their mouths came together and Craig thought he could drown in the taste of her as her tongue pressed through his lips.

Her free hand slipped into his hair as she held the bottle of wine in her other hand, and he felt the bottle against his back.

Craig cupped his hands over her bottom and she pressed against him harder. Before his legs gave out, because just having her pressed to him like that was making his knees wobble, he carried her to the couch.

He eased Rachel down on her back, and she set the bottle of wine on the floor as she pulled Craig down to her, her hand gripping the front of his shirt.

The strain in Craig's pants was a not-so-subtle reminder that the woman under him, currently unbuttoning his shirt, had a control over him that no other woman had. Ten years disappeared, and as Rachel pressed her hand to his bare chest, he remembered just how hard his heart had pounded the first time they'd been together.

A smile formed on her lips as she pushed his shirt away. "Your heart rate is a little fast," she teased, lifting her lips to his chest and pressing a kiss to his skin.

"You have always had a tendency to make that happen."

Her smile grew wider. "Have I?"

"You don't remember?"

She began to work on the button of his pants. "Oh, I remember. I'm woman enough now to say that I seduced you the first time."

And his heart rate kicked up a little more. "That's how you remember it?"

"Honey, I'd spent years planning that first night. If I were going to lose my virginity to anyone, it was going to be you. I was just lucky enough that I piqued your interest."

Craig eased himself back and looked down at her. "You have no idea how I felt for you back then, do you? Please tell me you don't think I was in it just for sex."

The air around them grew thicker and Rachel propped herself up on her elbows. "For years I convinced myself that's what it was. But looking up into your eyes now, I think we shared more than that. I was in love with you, Craig. I have never had feelings for anyone else like that."

Craig lowered himself again, propping himself on his forearms. "I loved you too. I didn't show it well, but I thought we would be forever. I knew in time your father would forgive me, but I had to prove myself to him—and me."

"You loved me?"

"I did. I told you that didn't I?"

Her eyes had grown damp. "You did, but hearing you

remember it that way..." She swallowed a sharp breath. "You have no idea what that means to me."

Craig pressed a kiss to her lips and lingered there. "Maybe we should have a few more discussions about this before we get all tangled up."

Rachel worried her bottom lip, lifting her hands to cup his face. "I don't think I'd like that at all."

Craig narrowed his gaze on her and she smiled up at him.

She licked her lips. "I think I'd like to finish what we started. Have some dinner. Do it again, and again, and again," she emphasized her words with a nip on his lips. "Then I'd like you to spend the night in my bed, and tomorrow I'll make you breakfast."

"You're making an appealing case."

"And I promise you. Tomorrow morning, while I'm only wearing that shirt I just pulled from you, you can ask me anything you'd like. We can spend all day filling in the holes of the past ten years."

Craig leaned in and accepted the deep kiss she gave him. The heat in the room increased again, and so did the tightness in his pants.

"Okay," he managed as he eased back and off the couch. Reaching for her hand, he pulled her to her feet. "I'll agree to your terms, but let's do this in your bedroom. You deserve better than what I would have given you a decade ago. You deserve to have this done right."

Rachel wrapped her arm around his neck as he swept up her legs and held her against him.

"Upstairs," she said as she took possession of his mouth.

It would be a miracle if they made it to her bed, he thought as he walked blindly through the house and up the stairs.

CHAPTER 18

C raig rolled to his back, his breath labored, the sheet cold on his skin, the room void of all light except what peeked around the door frame. Rachel reached for his hand, and pressed a kiss to his fingers.

They'd done it. They'd moved this—whatever it was—to the next level. Ten years had disappeared between them.

From the moment they'd hit the landing at the top of the stairs, clothes had been discarded. Kisses had wandered over skin. The sheets had been twisted up and knocked to the floor.

The room was dark, but Craig thought he could see a glow surround them, which had to be from the electricity that buzzed between them.

"That was incredible," Rachel said on a labored breath. "It's so much better as an adult." She laughed, but that squeezed in Craig's chest.

"You have done this since, haven't you?" he had to ask.

"Of course." Rachel rolled, propping herself up on her elbow. "But you don't forget your first." She traced her finger down his arm. "I'm going to go check on dinner."

"I'll be down in a moment," Craig said as he watched her

crawl from the bed and walk out of the room, still naked, only the glow of the light from the hallway illuminating her perfect body.

He heard the dogs scurry when she hit the bottom of the stairs, she spoke to them softly, and then it was quiet again.

Craig tucked his hands under his head and looked up at the ceiling. She'd been right, it was much better as adults, he thought. But then their first time together was etched in his head, and he remembered having taken a great deal of patience with her then. He had been fully aware of the risk and responsibility.

Now, years later, he was in her bed again and they were hiding from no one.

Craig heard her whistling and it made him smile. It did something to him to know he'd made her happy.

Rolling to the side of the bed, he sat up and placed his feet on the floor. A week ago, being with a woman wasn't on his mind. Now he wondered where this was going to go. They had a history, though short in the scheme of things. They had hurt feelings, broken promises, and secrets too.

The song she whistled turned into a song she began to sing. He supposed the reason he hadn't thought about women in a long time, was because the one singing downstairs was always filling his head.

Craig stood, picked up his pants, and pulled them on. His shirt was downstairs, and he supposed he could go out and get his bag now. It looked like they were on the same page for him staying overnight.

RACHEL DANCED THROUGH THE KITCHEN, the dogs always at her feet. She'd pulled open the oven and checked on the lasagna. It would be ready the moment Craig was.

She took the salad mix from the refrigerator, opened it, and poured it into a bowl. And even the act of it made her smile. Or perhaps it was the buzzing in her body that just hadn't stopped.

Craig Turner had been in her bed again, and everything in her world seemed a little lighter. Her mother would get over it, when she found out, and so would her brother. The voice of her father, the one that rang in her ears, would soon subside too, she thought.

In time, everything she'd ever wanted she would have. Hadn't she been planning this since she was fifteen?

"You look damn sexy in my shirt," Craig's voice behind her had her turning from the counter.

God, he was sexy standing there, leaned against the doorjamb in nothing but a pair of unbuttoned jeans.

"I found this on the floor," she said tugging at the sleeves of the shirt which she had buttoned at the wrists. "I hope you don't mind."

Craig licked his lips as he shook his head. "I don't mind at all."

"Dinner just needs to be served."

Craig nodded. "I'll run out to my car and get my bag, unless you want to relinquish that shirt."

Rachel shook her head. "Not until you have to leave, and even then I might reconsider."

He watched her for another moment before he retreated toward the door.

Rachel let out a slow breath. It would be easy to tell him she still loved him, but that would be irresponsible—nearly as irresponsible as having sex with him a week after her father's funeral. And she was smarter than that now. Love was bigger than crushes and empty promises, which was what they'd had when they were younger. Now love encompassed pasts, futures, and how he would deal with her shedding all of her secrets—in time.

Maybe a night with Coach's daughter had appealed to him, and all she was was a quick roll in the sack. She had to be ready for that. But when she thought about him telling her he hadn't only been in it for the sex, that he'd loved her back then, she had to assume his being there was because it meant more to him than just her offering.

She heard the front door close, and a moment later Craig was in the kitchen, this time with a Colorado Avalanche T-shirt on.

"Just for the record, it's too cold to go outside barefoot and shirtless," he joked and she turned from him so he couldn't see her face.

"Plates are in that far cupboard," she said as she opened the refrigerator and pulled out salad dressings.

As he took down the plates, and she closed the door to the refrigerator, they turned at the same time so they were facing each other.

She saw the flash in his eyes when he'd looked into hers.

"What's wrong?" he asked, setting the plates on the table and moving back to her. "You look like you might cry."

Rachel shook her head. "I've just thought of this for a long time. Now it's here and I don't know how it's going to end."

Craig took the dressings from her, set them on the table, and drew her into him. "I thought we were going to discuss that over breakfast."

"You really want to stay until breakfast?"

"I really do."

"You're not here just because it's a conquest?"

Craig eased back and looked down into her eyes. "I'm not a kid anymore. Rach, I wouldn't be here if I didn't feel something for you. I'm not that guy. I believe in relationships. I believe in rekindling ones that once meant something. I'm into you."

She let out the breath she was holding. "I got worked up over it. That's all."

"I see that. I wish you hadn't, because now I'll worry about it."

Rachel wrapped her arms around him and rested her cheek to his chest. "We'll talk about it tomorrow."

CHAPTER 19

They sat in her small kitchen, at her small table, their chairs pushed together. It was more intimate than any date in any restaurant could be.

The two dogs rested in their dog bed, Rover tucked in next to Clyde, who snored softly.

"You're a good cook," Craig said as he took another bite of the lasagna she had made. "I can hold my own, but I'm a sucker for carryout."

"Pizza is as close to carryout as I usually get. I like to cook."

"That I remember about you," he said as he tucked a loose strand of her hair behind her ear. "I vividly remember you always in the kitchen with your mother. And there was always a place for me at the counter, where I would sit and watch you both."

Rachel rested her head against his shoulder. "I remember. I was fifteen the first time you sat there watching us, and the rest of the team was in the basement playing pool."

"I hadn't even realized they'd left the room," he admitted.

Rachel sat up, and took another bite of her lasagna. "It was the first time I really noticed you," she said. "Before then, you melded in with the team. Hal and Theo would hang with you guys, and I was told to stay upstairs. But when you hung around, I noticed."

Craig picked up his wine and sipped. "That was a long time ago."

Rachel set down her fork and turned to him. "I know I was only fifteen then, but you taking the time to get to know me made me want to make you mine."

Craig rested his arms on the table and scanned her sincere eyes. "I hope I was never," he considered his words, "unkind to you. I didn't realize you had an interest until you were much older."

Rachel placed her hand on his arm. "Oh, I was interested," she said as she moved from her chair, eased Craig back, and moved to straddle him on his chair. She wrapped her arms around his neck and pressed a kiss to his lips. "And you were never unkind," she confirmed. "That's probably why I was in love with you for so long."

Running his hands up her back, underneath the fabric of his shirt, which she wore, he sunk into the kiss she continued. Her tongue slipped against his, and he knew right where it was going to lead.

"Our dinner is going to get cold," he mumbled into her hair as her lips moved from his and skimmed his neck.

"I'm not hungry," she admitted as her lips moved to his ear. "Take me out to the couch. I don't need a bed."

THE AIR WAS cool in the early morning as the sun began to brighten the horizon. Rachel lay curled up next to him, his shirt, now a wrinkled mess, still on her, though open. Her hair splayed across his chest, and her breath steady against his skin.

Craig ran his thumb over her knuckles of the hand that rested on his chest. And in that moment, he knew that the feeling he was embracing was what they'd both chased all those years ago. Contentment, peace, togetherness, and he knew in his heart there was love. What was to be seen was whether the love he was feeling was for the torrid romance of the past, or if it was for the woman, who in one week, had turned his world upside down, again.

When she stirred, he found that he held his breath. Rachel Diaz had been a constant thought in his mind for a decade. They had used the words once, professing their love to one another. Sure, when he'd moved on and got married, he'd said them again to someone else. But Rachel had been his first love, he knew that. If she hadn't been, she certainly wouldn't have occupied so much of his mind.

"What are you thinking about?" her voice was soft as it broke the silence.

"You."

She turned so that he could see the smile that formed on her full lips. "I'm right here. What's to think about?"

"What we had before."

Her eyes slowly opened and she looked up at him. "I think about that a lot."

Craig brushed the strands of hair that lay across her face away with his fingertips. "I often wonder if I was man enough to wait for you. I thought I was. Then my father came along and filled my head with hateful nonsense, and your father said I wasn't to see you again..." he didn't want to continue.

"I get it now," she said propping her chin on her hand, which still rested on his chest. "I was mad for a lot of years." She bit down hard on her bottom lip. "I know he was protecting me now. And, he was probably protecting you too. If you'd have waited for me to finish college, you wouldn't have gone on to live your life."

"We talked about marriage once, do you remember?"

Rachel let out a small giggle. "I'm surprised you remember.

Aren't men supposed to not be sentimental about things like that?"

"I'm kind of a sap," he admitted. "I remember it."

She circled her fingers in the small tuft of hair on his chest. "I remember that I had told my parents I was at Catherine's house. But I was with you. We spent the night in your car."

Craig groaned. "Completely unromantic."

"No. It was memorable. But I remember you saying you wanted to marry me."

"I did say that."

Rachel lifted her head and her eyes locked with his. "You have no idea how much that meant to me."

"You didn't write that off as someone who was just trying to have their way with you?"

"Is that what you were doing?"

"Not in the least."

She smiled. "Then see, I was right to keep the sentiment close to my heart."

Craig ran his hand over her hair. "So, what do you see happening here, with us now?"

Rachel shrugged her shoulders. "I seduced you again."

"Is that what you did?"

She nodded slowly as she licked her lips. "Now I'll just have to see if you answer my calls next week."

"Why wouldn't I answer your calls?"

"You might just think this is something I'm doing in mourning."

The word hurt. She was in mourning, so was he. Was that what they were doing? Were they just finding comfort?

"I'll answer your calls," he promised.

She lifted, nipped his lips with a kiss, and then rolled off the bed. Standing before him, she buttoned up the shirt she'd taken possession of. "Then I'll remain optimistic that I can make you fall in love with me again."

CHAPTER 20

When Craig hit the bottom step, Clyde immediately was at his feet, dragging his leash along. He looked up to see Rachel and Rover walking toward him.

She'd changed into a pair of leggings, a sweatshirt that had a bright yellow CU logo on it, and her sneakers. Her hair was piled on top of her head in a floppy bun, and her face had been cleaned of the mascara that had darkened her eyes during sleep. She looked refreshed.

He, on the other hand, had seen his reflection in the bathroom mirror. The thought that he'd need to shave hadn't even crossed his mind when he'd packed that overnight bag.

Rachel lifted on her toes and pressed a kiss to his cheek before running her hand over his whiskers. "I like this."

"My unshaven face?"

She shrugged. "You forget, you didn't have all of this when I last kissed you. You didn't have that hair on your chest either."

"You have a good memory."

"It was seared in there pretty good," she said smiling. "I have to take the dogs out. Do you want to join us?"

How could he turn down the three sets of dark eyes that had turned up to look at him?

Craig slipped on his jacket and took Clyde's leash as they headed out the door.

RACHEL LOCKED the door and turned to see Craig standing there with her dogs. She didn't think she'd ever tire of the sight. The man, who taught and coached just as her father had, with his mussed hair and dark eyes shadowed from lack of sleep, still stirred her up.

Inhaling the brisk morning air, she tried to steady her heart. It had probably been a risk to welcome Craig back into her life, especially at such a vulnerable time. When her father had passed, she wondered if Craig would attend the funeral—she'd hoped he would. There was comfort in thinking he'd be there, and it seemed to have gotten her through the stress of it all.

More than likely she'd set herself up for heartbreak when she'd asked him to meet her that night. She couldn't help herself.

She was in control this time and had the emotional tools to work through it.

But what if it didn't end in heartbreak? What if it worked out?

They'd once loved one another. Some of that hadn't left her heart. Was there still love in his?

He'd said it wasn't just sex. He'd loved her once.

"Doing okay?" he asked looking at her.

Rachel smiled at him as she picked up Rover's leash. "I'm doing great," she said as she reached for Craig's hand and interlaced their fingers, a gesture she found more intimate than sex itself.

~

CRAIG PARKED his car in his garage just past noon on Saturday, and rested his head against the back of the seat. He closed his eyes for a moment.

His weekend with Rachel had been cut short when her mother called while they were on their walk with the dogs, and wanted her to come by, as her father's sister had dropped by and her mother didn't want to be alone with her. Apparently, Hal wasn't readily available.

Rachel had been overly apologetic, but Craig assured her it was okay. There were moments he forgot the Diaz family was still in mourning. And that formed a ball of guilt in his gut.

He didn't feel as if he'd pushed Rachel into anything, and perhaps their night together had helped her cope. But the lingering question in his mind was had they just finished something, or started something.

Craig's eyes shot open when something hit the back of his car, and when he spun to look, Bruce stood behind his car with a look of satisfaction on his face.

Craig pushed open his door and stepped out of the car.

Bruce's laughter echoed through the old garage. "What the hell, buddy? Asleep in your car?"

"Long night," Craig admitted as he opened the backdoor to his car and took out his bag.

"Looks like you had a sleepover elsewhere? Of course, the fact that you're sleeping in your car means you didn't get any sleep at all." Bruce's brow rose. "Anyone I know?"

"I think I need a pot of coffee before I answer that." Craig closed the door to the garage and walked to the house.

Bruce let out a low hum. "You haven't been around her in a decade, and in one week you already landed Coach's daughter?"

Craig stuck the key in the lock and turned it. "Don't cheapen it," he said and heard the bite in his words. "I guess it's a touchy subject."

"Didn't go well?" Bruce asked as Craig pushed open the door and proceeded to drop his bag and hang up his coat.

Bruce followed, closing the door behind him.

Craig moved right to the coffee maker, filled the pot with water from the sink, and poured it into the machine.

He took a moment to formulate what he wanted to tell Bruce, then figured he'd just spill it all. What did he have to lose? It wasn't kissing and telling, or was it? It wasn't as if Bruce couldn't figure it all out on his own, nor would he cheapen it, well he would for the sake of razzing Craig, but that would be it.

And, it wasn't as if it would hurt Rachel. They weren't kids. This was more. Or, as he'd considered earlier, was it more or over?

Bruce pulled out a chair from the small kitchen table and sat down. "You're not going to give me details?"

"I'm just figuring them out myself," Craig admitted as he scooped the grounds from the can, added them to the filter, and pressed start on the machine. "I don't know if we started something or finished it," he said turning to face Bruce. "And yes, my night was with Rachel Diaz, the woman, and certainly not the teenager."

Bruce shook his head. "How long are you going to be living in this house?"

The question took Craig off guard. "What the hell does that mean?"

"It means I think you started something, not ended it. You've had a thing for her since she was a kid. As gross as that sounds, but I don't mean it that way. She got in your head back then, and the minute she called out your name at the funeral, she got in there again."

"Not just my head, man."

"I know that. That's what I'm saying. Back then it was taboo, off limits, and a risk. Now you can be as free with it as you want, but seeing you spinning it in your head, as you are, it means one thing, friend."

"What's that?"

"You're in love with her again—still. You're going to twist it all up until it makes you sick. You're going to feel guilt about it because it goes against the rules that Coach set out for the two of you. You're going to think that everything that happened to her back then was your fault, and you're going to blame yourself forever, until you push her away."

Craig heard the sound of the coffee brewing behind him, but now it was the blood pumping through his veins that thudded in his ears.

"What do you mean I'll feel guilty about what happened to her back then? What exactly happened to her?"

CHAPTER 21

Rachel brewed a pot of coffee and set cookies out on a plate for her aunt and her mother. She wasn't quite sure why her mother had needed her there. Her mother and aunt had always been as close as sisters, but it seemed in the absence of her father, Rachel's mother was intimidated by his sister.

Her aunt Dorothy smiled up at Rachel as she carried in the plate of cookies and the pot of coffee. She set them on the table and then filled each of the coffee mugs. "Can I get you both something else?"

Her mother shook her head and her aunt's eyes gazed up softly at her. "Just come join us, dear. I'd love to catch up."

Rachel nodded, returned the coffee pot, and rejoined them carrying her own mug.

Her aunt took a cookie and bit into it. "You're still in the school system?" she asked Rachel.

"I am. I'm in a high school. It's satisfying work."

"I'm sure you're touching lives. You always were good at listening and helping," she said kindly.

"I appreciate that."

Her mother picked up her coffee mug with shaky hands. "She was a Godsend after Theo died," she said before sipping her coffee.

Rachel felt the ache in her heart watching her mother still processing the loss of her son, and wasn't that only the start of it all, Rachel thought as she brushed her hands over the sleeves of her shirt.

Dorothy uncrossed her legs, and recrossed them, resting her hands on her knees. "Your daddy was proud of you, and your brother. He talked about you both all the time." She reached her hand to Rachel's mother's hand and covered it. "And you were his light," Dorothy assured her. "He was smitten the minute he met you. Oh, and Esther, he couldn't have found a better partner."

Rachel's mother lifted her tear-filled eyes. "Thank you. That's very kind of you."

"No, it's truth. I'm sorry Hal isn't here. I was hoping to get to see him too before I headed back home."

"He had things to take care of," her mother's voice shook. "He'll be sorry he missed you."

Dorothy wrapped up her visit and Rachel walked her to her car.

"Your mama will be okay," she said as she opened the passenger door and set her purse on the seat. "I just wanted to make sure she was doing okay. I know my brother's passing affected a lot of people. It was nice to see that team he cared so much about at the funeral. Though, they're all grown men now."

The mention of the team had Rachel sucking in a breath. "They loved him very much."

Dorothy touched Rachel's arm. "And you're doing okay? I mean, oh hell, I don't know what I mean. You're a grown woman who is trained to take care of people in mourning and who are depressed. But I guess it's okay to ask if you're okay."

"It's okay to ask. My career is what helped me along the way, and now I have the tools to get through all of this."

"Every time I read about some young person in the paper, I think of Theo and you," she said softly giving Rachel's arm a squeeze. "I want you to know, from the depths of my heart, I'm so proud of you. I know that you've saved lives doing what you do. I wish we all had someone on our side, as your students do."

Rachel batted back tears. "Thank you."

"Now, let's not be so serious for a moment. Are you seeing anyone? You're such a beautiful woman, you should be dating, if you're not."

Now Rachel laughed and the tears dried. "I'm seeing someone. It's new," she said, not wanting to draw attention to the fact that she'd stirred things up from the past.

Her aunt grinned. "Your mama doesn't know that yet, does she?"

"Not yet."

"Make sure he takes good care of you," she warned. "You only deserve the best."

Dorothy leaned in and kissed Rachel on the cheek before walking to the other side of her car, climbing in, and driving away.

Rachel watched until she'd turned the corner, and then she walked back inside the house.

Her mother still sat on the sofa sipping her coffee and Rachel could see her hands still shook.

"Mama, are you okay?"

"Fine. I'm fine." She set the mug down using both hands. "Thank you for coming over."

"Why were you so worried about having Aunt Dorothy here?"

"I'm just over company, sweetheart. I've had people dropping by all week." Her mother's eyes widened. "I don't mean you and Hal, though. I enjoy you being here."

Rachel smiled. "I know."

"I hope she didn't upset you by talking about you and Theo. I always worry when someone lumps you in the same conversation."

"Mama, I've worked very hard to make that part of my life part of my story. It's the catalyst to my life's work. When someone mentions it, I can deal with it."

Her mother reached for her hand and gave it a squeeze as Rachel sat down next to her on the sofa. "I'm so proud of you. I wish Theo would have had your strength."

Rachel wasn't sure she would call what she'd overcome strength, though anyone else in the same situation she'd tell them the same thing.

"I appreciate that you think I'm strong."

"I've never known anyone stronger and more in charge of their destiny."

Rachel put her other hand on top of her mother's. "Do you still have a freezer full of food? Maybe we can decide what to have for dinner and I can stay the night with you."

Her mother's lips curled into a smile. "I'd appreciate that, but I know you need your time too."

"I've gone out to dinner a few times this week and spent the evening with a friend. I'm doing okay."

"I'm glad to hear that." Her mother picked up her mug again, and Rachel noticed that she was steadier. "So, tell me, who did you spend your evening with?"

CHAPTER 22

Craig wasn't imagining it, Bruce's eyes had gone wide and the color had drained from his face.

"Man, listen, this isn't for me to be discussing with you casually. I was just coming by to tell you that I turned over my lease and I can move in this week, if the offer is still open." Bruce's voice shook as he spoke.

"The space is yours, and it doesn't matter what the hell you tell me." Craig pulled out the other chair and sat down, his hands clasped together in the center of the table. "Let's circle back to me feeling guilty."

Bruce ran his tongue over his teeth. "Listen, Rachel had a hard time after we graduated. That's all. I thought you knew that."

"I knew she gave up all her scholarships and went to school out of state."

Had he actually seen Bruce wince at that?

Craig laid his hands out flat on the table. "That's not what happened? She didn't mention anything different to me when I brought it up the other night."

"Seriously, I don't think I'm the one that should be having this conversation with you."

"Well, you are. So tell me what the hell happened to her."

Bruce eased back in his chair and studied Craig for a long moment. "Finding her brother did a real job on her."

"As it would to anyone who walked in to see their brother hanging from his neck in the bathroom. They got her help for that."

Bruce chuckled. "As if, at the tender age of seventeen, you just forget that shit and move on," he said easing his arms on the table. "Man, she was in counseling, she was medicated, and the minute she turned eighteen, she got caught having sex with you. She was pretty messed up."

"She was dealing with great trauma. And us getting caught was stupid. We let our guard down."

"They were on to you from the minute she was of age. I'm surprised you didn't get caught for months."

Craig ran his hand over his face. "She told me last night that she'd planned her seduction of me for years."

That made Bruce laugh. "I wouldn't doubt it. There wasn't a guy on that team that wasn't interested in Rachel Diaz, myself included. But she never had eyes for anyone but you."

Craig rested his elbows on the table. "Seems odd that you're telling me this story then if I was the one that held all the cards."

"Yeah, but you were too stupid to hold what was dear, and I mean that in the sincerest way you can to anyone who was in their early twenties, whose dad waited until his graduation to ever reach out to him, and who knew he had four years to wait for the girl of his dreams."

Craig stood from the table, pulled down two coffee mugs, and set them on the counter. He turned to the corner cabinet, opened it, and took down the whiskey. This conversation was going to need something stronger than coffee.

He didn't ask any more questions until he had the mugs filled with coffee, whiskey added, and had set them on the table. When he took his seat, he drew in a deep breath.

"I know about her medications and her counselors. I was there for that, remember? You don't find your brother after he commits suicide and not get the help you need. Trust me, she cried on my shoulder a lot," he confirmed and Bruce nodded.

"And then when we graduated, your dad got in your head, and you weren't good for anyone."

Craig considered that this was the kind of conversation that ended friendships, or in his case, the kind that made one friend want to punch the other right in the jaw.

He sipped his coffee, and could admit he'd added way too much whiskey, but he was going to drink it—all of it.

"My dad is a son-of-a-bitch. Let's leave it at that."

Bruce nodded again. "Sure. We can leave it at that. Only when he got in your head to tell you what a piece of shit you were, and obviously he would know right? I mean, he skipped out on your entire life." Bruce paused for a moment. "But his opportune timing turned you into a son-of-a-bitch. You didn't have time for us. You didn't have time for Coach. And you certainly didn't have time for Rachel."

The shittiest part of Bruce's whole story was that it was true. Craig had become the kind of friend that people wanted to forget. His father had gotten into his head, and if Coach hadn't vouched for him to get that first job, he was sure things would have gone the other way—the wrong way.

Craig took a long sip of the whiskey-laced coffee and blew out a hot breath when he was done. He tried to remember if he'd done anything or said anything to Rachel before she moved away. No, he couldn't come up with anything, and there lay the problem. He'd simply given up on her—and himself.

"I walked away from Rachel," he admitted.

"You walked away from all of us. Alex tried to step in and befriend her."

The very thought of it had the hairs on the back of Craig's

neck standing up. "I step aside and Alex moves the hell in? What the fu…"

"He didn't move in. Drop the act, dick." Bruce sat back and thew his hands up. "Okay, maybe he did move in for that reason. I don't know. What I know is that after you left, Rachel went down a different path. Her depression got worse. She was drinking and medicating." Bruce drew in a long breath. "And cutting."

"Cutting? Cutting what?"

"Herself, you asshole."

And with that, it felt as if the wind had been knocked out of his lungs. Bruce was right. Guilt filled his entire body and paralyzed him in the chair.

Bruce leaned in and wrapped his hands around his mug. "They got her help, but before she was supposed to leave for school, she tried to commit suicide too."

The thudding in Craig's ears grew louder as the blood rushed through his veins. Certainly he hadn't heard that right. No, Rachel knew first hand how devastating it was to find her brother and what his death did to her and her family. There was no way any of this was true.

Bruce took another sip of his coffee and then pushed it away. "So they put her in a facility to get her help, where she wouldn't hurt herself anymore."

"She didn't go away to school?"

Bruce shook his head. "Damn, man, I thought you knew all of this."

He sure as hell didn't know any of it. But if he had, would anything have changed? And now that he did know, what was he supposed to do with the information and the feelings he had for Rachel now that they were all jumbled up with the guilt?

CHAPTER 23

The house was quiet. Craig sat on his couch, feet propped up on the coffee table, and watched the flicker of the news on his TV. He didn't even have the sound on because there was enough noise in his head replaying the conversation with Bruce.

Craig lifted the beer in his hand to his lips and contemplated what Rachel had been going through when he was starting his adult life.

Bruce had been right, Craig was filled with guilt and now that toyed with his feelings.

He lowered the bottle and swirled the liquid left inside.

When his phone buzzed on the table next to him, he didn't pick it up. It had been going off for the past hour, and like a gutless coward, he didn't want to look at it just in case it was Rachel. He just wasn't ready for that yet.

Rolling his head from side to side, he tried to loosen the knots that had formed in his shoulders.

Did any of the information he now had change how he felt for Rachel? Then again, in a week, did he know how he felt about her?

Craig finished off the beer. Of course he knew. He'd always known. Rachel was the one true love of his life. Even marriage hadn't removed that knowledge, nor had it worked out. He hadn't wanted family and forever with Colleen, but when he thought about it with Rachel, it was always in his mind as the whole package.

Resting his head back against the chair, he closed his eyes. He'd like to think that his friends no longer thought he was a son-of-a-bitch. He'd changed. Coach had thought enough of him, even after everything Craig had done to prove him wrong, to vouch for him and help start his career. So why was he going to hold Rachel's past against her?

Craig picked up the phone and scrolled through the messages.

There was one from a colleague asking if he could cover a class for her. Another from Bruce checking on him and apologizing for having been such an ass. He'd reply to that one first. There was no need for Bruce's apology. Another text from Alex made it clear that Bruce had already talked to everyone, so maybe Craig wouldn't text Bruce back first.

And the last text was from Toby looking for some intel on Bruce. Maybe he'd finally asked Toby for a job.

He chuckled and began to reply to that text first, pretending that it didn't bother him that Rachel hadn't been one of those texts.

As soon as he sent the text to Toby that vouched for Bruce, his phone rang in his hand. That pounding in his chest resumed as he looked down at the screen and saw Rachel's name come up.

Taking a long, cleansing breath, he answered.

"Hey," his voice was nearly a whisper.

"Did I interrupt you?" She asked and Craig leaned forward, resting his elbows on his knees.

"No. I was just returning some texts."

"I'm sorry about our weekend. I guess I'm going to stay with Mom tonight. She seems to need the company."

"Of course. I'm sure things are hard for her right now."

He heard the sounds of her walking and a door closing. "I had a really nice time last night. I just wanted you to know."

Craig sat back. "I'm glad. I had a nice time too."

"I just wanted to clear something up. In case, well," she let out a breath, "in case you think I'm using you to push past my mourning."

Craig ran his fingers over his stubbled chin. "Okay." He drew out the word.

"I've thought of you all the time since we last saw each other. You were the first man I ever loved, and I kept that with me all this time."

"Rach..."

"I'm not saying it to justify this weekend. I'm saying it because you need to hear it. I don't know where you are in your life, relationship wise. I mean, maybe it was just a weekend to you, and that's okay," she quickly added. "But it meant a lot to me, and I'd really like to keep seeing you."

Craig swallowed hard and realized that ball of guilt had risen from his chest to his throat and it choked him. "What does your mom think of that idea?"

"I didn't discuss it with my mom, or my brother. It's none of their business," her words grew sharper, though not any louder. "I'd understand if you don't..."

"I do," he cut her off, but it had come from his heart and not his head. "I do want to see you more. I've missed you, Rach."

He heard the sigh, which he assumed was relief. "Good." She laughed. "I guess we jumped right over the dating and getting to know you part, didn't we?"

"I guess we did."

"I'm crazy busy this next week, but I could bring dinner over on Wednesday. Do you mind if my dogs come for a visit?"

"I don't mind at all," he said and then winced. "Wait, Bruce is moving in on Wednesday."

"He's moving in with you?"

"Yeah. He's out of work and needs to downsize. I have a bachelor pad in the basement and offered it to him."

There was a moment of pause. "I'll bring dinner for him too. It'll be nice to catch up."

"No pressure."

"Nope, you all were important to Dad, and to me. I'd like to catch up."

"I'll see you Wednesday then?" he asked.

"I'll see you Wednesday. Oh, and Craig, thanks for the shirt. It's my favorite," she said before the line went dead.

Craig looked at his phone and smiled. They'd have to talk about it at some time. If they were going to make a go of this thing they'd started, they were going to have to fill in the blanks.

A fresh start. Yeah, that's what it was, a fresh start.

He lifted his phone again and found Bruce's number. Perhaps he should warn him before he was blindsided on Wednesday.

CHAPTER 24

Rachel opened the back door for the dogs, and they eagerly ran out into her mother's yard. Clyde pranced around the banks of snow that still remained, but Rover dove right into them.

She laughed as she watched their antics, closing the door against the cold and moving to the coffee maker. It was late when they'd gone to bed. She found comfort that her mother had wanted to stay up into the wee hours of the morning talking and watching old movies, but Rachel knew she'd need to catch up on sleep at some point. She was still tired from the night she'd shared with Craig. They hadn't gotten much sleep either.

Rachel made her coffee and a piece of toast. She wasn't sure when her mother would come downstairs, so she'd eat a little something now, and she and her mother could make breakfast later.

The dogs yipped at one another out back, and Rachel smiled. Perhaps she should have asked Craig if he had a fenced in yard.

"What are you thinking of so early?" her mother's voice broke through the silence.

Rachel lifted her smile to her mother. "The dogs."

"Maybe I should think about getting one now that Dad is gone. He never wanted to hassle with them, but it would be good company, I think."

"I think you're right. We could go to the shelter tomorrow after school and look if you'd like."

Her mother sat down at the table and waited for the coffee to finish brewing. When it had, Rachel poured them each a cup and joined her mother at the table.

"I think I'll wait on a dog," her mother picked back up the conversation where she'd left off. "But maybe this summer."

"I think that sounds like a good time to get one. You could go for walks."

"I would like that."

Rachel stood and retrieved her mother's creamer from the refrigerator and slid it in front of her mother. "I made some toast, but we could make something else."

"I'd take some toast," she said pouring the creamer into her mug. "Would you hand me a spoon?"

Rachel opened the drawer, pulled out a spoon, and handed it to her mother. As she did, her mother took hold of her wrist and examined her arm.

"You've had more work done," she said admiring the sleeve of tattoos that Rachel wore on her arm.

It always choked Rachel up when her mother looked at her arm as she was. She was grateful that she admired the artwork, but she couldn't help but wonder if she was looking deeper, trying to find all of the scars that the deep blue ocean mural covered up. Even though she'd covered her arm in tattoos, she usually wore long sleeves, but this morning she wore a tank top.

"Just the starfish," Rachel said as she pulled back her arm. "I went in the day after Daddy died."

"He was your star."

"He was," Rachel admitted as she turned to the toaster and slid in two more pieces of bread.

Retrieving the butter and the jelly from the refrigerator, she gave her mother the slices of toast she'd made earlier. "I'll wait for the others."

Her mother took the spoon from her coffee, wiped it off on a napkin from the holder, and dipped it into the butter. She looked up at Rachel as she spread the butter on the toast. "You never did tell me which friend you'd spent the evening with the other night."

Rachel turned back to the toaster and set the warm pieces of toast on a plate. "Didn't I?"

"No," her mother drew out the word and Rachel wondered if she should. "Do you not want to tell me?"

Rachel took her plate to the table, stared at it, and pushed it away. "I spent the evening with Craig Turner," she said, folding her arms on the table and watching her mother nearly pierce the toast with the spoon.

"Oh," her mother replied, her voice shaky. She set down her toast and twisted the napkin in her hands. "You had dinner with him?"

"Yes, I did."

"That was nice. He was one of your father's favorite players."

"He was."

Her mother picked up her mug, but her hands shook so much that the coffee spilled over the edge. Rachel picked up another napkin and wiped it away.

"Oh, Rachel," her mother began to sob. "Why? Why do this?"

"Why do what?"

"You promised your father you wouldn't see him again."

"And that was a decade ago, and I had a lot more going on than just my affection for Craig Turner."

"He used you."

"He did not," she argued. "Who said he used me?"

"You were young."

"I was of age," she reminded her.

"Just." Her mother picked up the toast and bit down hard. "It showed disrespect for your father."

"He was never anything but respectful to me. Craig is not the problem here."

"Really?" Her mother grabbed her arm. "The paint doesn't cover what happened to you."

"Why was that Craig's fault?"

"He broke his promise to you and your father."

"*We* broke a promise to dad. Besides, he had his own issues," her voice was rising.

"Which became your problem."

Rachel balled her fists. "He didn't have anything to do with his father," she reminded her mother. "His father's attacking Daddy like that was…"

"The sure mark of a coward." Her mother's voice shook.

"Craig didn't know his father did that. I'm not sure he knows now. His father had set out to ruin him."

The angry tears stung Rachel's eyes as her mother wiped at her own tears. "He pushed you into that depression that…" she sucked in a breath, "that…" She stopped and pointed toward Rachel's arm.

Rachel looked down at the extensive tattoo that covered her arm—her scars. "This is because of Theo, damnit!" She pushed back from the table, angry that her mother had laid all the blame on Craig. "What Theo did was a selfish, prick thing to do to our family!" She shouted and her mother stood.

A moment later Rachel felt the sting of the slap that came across her cheek, and then her mother crumpled into a ball at the table, sobbing.

Rachel held her hand to her cheek before sinking down next to her mother. She gathered her in her arms and held her tight. There was still processing that needed to be had even twelve years later.

Her training taught her to pity Theo, and to understand that he hid his trauma and depression. But at the same time, she hated him for what he'd done to her and her family. Finding the lifeless body of someone you loved and looked up to was never something someone would get over. He'd had that choice. It just so happened that the trauma of that moment fell on Rachel.

But how convenient for her family that could pin her dive into depression, drinking, cutting, and suicidal thoughts on Craig so they didn't have to actually put blame on Theo for the devastation he caused his family.

CHAPTER 25

R ay eyeballed the pickup truck parked in Craig's driveway. "There is no way in hell all of this is going to fit in that basement," he said as Bruce handed him a beer, and then handed one to Craig from a cooler he'd brought with him and had set on the lawn.

Bruce gestured to the truck with his beer. "Now, I look at this truck and think I'm some sorry bastard. Everything I own fits into one extended bed pickup truck."

Craig and Ray laughed collectively as they each took a pull from their beers.

Craig nudged Ray. "We shouldn't give him a hard time. He's moving up. He's got new digs and a new job all in one week."

Bruce shook his head. "And when I find out which of you sons-of-bitches went behind my back and told Toby I was desperate, I'll kick your ass."

"No one told me," Toby's voice came from behind them and they watched as he walked from his BMW, which he'd parked out front, up the incline of the driveway. "I need you in my organization," he told Bruce. "You'll be a welcome asset."

"Shit," Bruce huffed out the word. "I was really looking forward to kicking someone's ass."

That warranted another laugh from them all. Bruce handed Toby the beer he'd opened, but had yet to drink from, and took another out of the cooler.

Toby sipped from the can. "Though, with a job, maybe you can buy something with some taste. What is this crap?" He looked at the can.

"It's free for those who help me move," Bruce explained. "Let's get this inside before we lose the sunlight and freeze our asses off."

Within an hour, the four men had carried all of Bruce's belongings into the house. They'd polished off the case of beer, and were now challenging each other to a rousing game of pool.

Toby lined up for a shot. "So fill me in. I heard rumor that you've already made a move on Coach's daughter," he said toward Craig as he made his shot and sunk two of his balls.

Craig watched him walk around the table with a cocky grin. "I didn't make a move. She asked me out. I went. And we went again."

Toby made another shot, only this time he missed. "So, you're dating?"

Bruce shook his head. "He's doing more than that," he said on a laugh as he lined up for his shot.

"You're all assholes," Craig said, finishing his beer.

Ray gave Craig a nudge. "In all seriousness. Fill us in."

Craig exchanged glances with Bruce, who shanked his shot. "Fine. I'm seeing Rachel."

Ray ran the chalk over the tip of his stick. "Seeing her?" he asked as he moved in to make his shot. "You're dating? Going to movies. Long walks in the park?"

"Sure."

Ray laughed as he missed his shot. "And some hot and heavy between the sheets?"

"None of your business."

Ray nodded. "Nuff said, I think."

"Hello?" the voice called from the top of the stairs. "Craig?"

The four men stopped, looked at each other, and then all heads turned to look at Craig, who felt the heat rise in his cheeks.

"I'll be right up," he said, setting his cue in the rack. "Shut up," he said scanning a look at all of them as he left them in the basement and ran up the steps.

Rachel was standing just inside the back door of his house, and he couldn't help but want to gather her up and plant a warm kiss on her lips. But, considering the company he was keeping, he refrained.

"I knocked on the front door, but no one answered. I hope you don't mind that I..."

"I don't mind." Now he moved in and pressed a quick kiss to her lips.

"I let the dogs in your yard. I'd meant to ask if you had a fenced yard, but luckily you do."

He looked out beyond her and watched as Rover explored and Clyde followed her.

"They look happy," he said, realizing he hadn't invited her further into the house.

"There's a lot of cars here. Do you have company?"

Craig looked down the stairs. "Everyone came to help Bruce move in. I should kick them out."

Rachel laughed. "Don't do that. I can come back some other time."

"No. We had plans."

She smiled and it brought a light to her eyes. "I made enchiladas. And you know, I can't just make a few. So I have enough to feed everyone."

This time he did move to her, gathered her in his arms, and planted a warm kiss to her lips. "Are you sure you want to put up with these asshats?" he asked, knowing full well they were straining to listen.

"Oh, I would love to make good with them. You never know when I'll need to move and could use help."

They both laughed when they heard the grumbling from the basement. Sure enough, they were listening.

"I'll go get the trays from my car," she said.

Craig heard the footsteps coming up behind him as Rachel walked back to her car.

Ray let out a sigh. "Do we have to behave ourselves now, Dad?" he teased.

"More than you ever have," Craig said, but meant it. He wasn't calm yet, having learned what he had when Bruce dumped the information about Rachel's past on him. If Bruce knew all of that, what did the other two know?

Now Ray rested his hand on Craig's shoulder. "We've got your back, pal," he said as he passed by him and followed Rachel to her car.

And Craig knew that was what he'd needed to hear. The years might have gotten away from them, but they all still had one another's backs.

With that, Craig followed Ray and Rachel out to her car to help her bring in the food she'd prepared.

CHAPTER 26

Craig had pulled out his folding table, and Bruce had brought his upstairs. Kitchen chairs and folding chairs encircled the tables, and the boys—men—who had once sat around Rachel's parents' kitchen table now joined together in Craig Turner's house.

She sat with her legs folded beneath her and listened to the men talk about their jobs, ex-wives, basketball, and that rounded the conversation to Rachel's father.

Bruce sat back in his chair and folded his napkin, and then refolded it. "Coach went to bat for me in the psych class I was failing," he said. "He marched into that professor's office, said I needed to pass that class, but on my own merits, and asked him what I needed to do." Bruce blew out a breath. "I was mortified, but the professor said he'd give me some time to do the test over because he respected the coach for caring that much about his players."

There was a collective sigh and Toby leaned in on his forearms. "Did you know he was my first investor?"

All eyes turned toward him and Rachel laughed. "My dad invested in your business?"

"One of my businesses," he chuckled. "In college I started a lawn service so I could stay in Boulder. He bought my first mower, and loaned me the rest of the money for the trimmer and the blower."

"My dad did that for you?" The tears began to sting her eyes, and Craig reached for her hand.

"He also hired me first. I told him that I would do your family's lawn for free, but he said that wasn't how you made money."

The first tear fell, and Rachel quickly brushed it away.

"I didn't mean to upset you," Toby said.

"It doesn't upset me. Look at you now. You have one of the biggest tech firms in the state—in the country. You always had a work ethic, and to think my dad helped get you started. You honor him by doing what you do now, and by remembering him."

Toby's cheeks had gone pink, and she knew he understood.

Ray crossed his arms in front of him and leaned back in his chair. "He helped me shop for tires for that old pickup I used to have. God, remember that beast?"

Craig nodded. "I remember pushing it out of numerous intersections when it died."

Bruce raised his hand. "I remember doing that too."

Craig gave Rachel's hand a squeeze. "He was always there for us. Even when my dad came back into my life. Coach sat me down and told me to be true to myself." He ran his fingers over his chin. "God, if only I'd listened."

Toby picked up a corn chip, broke it in half, and bit down on one of the pieces. "Imagine where you'd be if you'd listened to Coach. You severed ties, man. I don't mean to be a dick, but..."

"But I did," Craig admitted and ran his thumb over Rachel's knuckles.

She forced back the tears that wanted to fall.

Did Craig even know what damage his father had done? He'd crashed into Craig's life at a volatile time, spread his disdain, and then carried it into Rachel's home when he threatened her father.

And still, her father had gone to Craig and even helped get him started in his career.

Had her father fought for Craig's wellbeing only, or was he fighting for hers as well? She'd never know.

Rachel had taken to rebellion and depression in order to deal with the drama around her. She'd blamed Theo for her lot in life, and nearly had taken her own. But now knowing her family blamed Craig and his abandonment, and his father's insertion into their lives for her misguided ways, sitting there as they all reminisced had begun to make her ill.

Suddenly the room became so warm that the air in her lungs felt thick.

She pulled her hand from Craig's, untucked her legs from under her, and pushed back. "Excuse me," she said as she hurried down the hall to the bathroom she'd seen, and locked the door.

ALL EYES FOLLOWED Rachel as she ran out of the room.

Toby ran his hand over his forehead. "I think we crossed a line."

Craig shook his head. "No, it's just still fresh. If anyone crossed a line, it was me a decade ago."

Ray began to gather the plates and stack them together. "I think it's time for us to go." He stood and the others helped to clean up the table.

They set the plates in the sink, threw the bottles in the recycle bin, and at the back door, Toby and Ray hugged Craig and Bruce goodbye. Then, Bruce disappeared down the stairs.

Craig stood in the kitchen for another moment, gathering his thoughts. He'd heard the door open, but Rachel didn't head toward the kitchen, so he went to find her.

She was sitting on his bed, when he found her. Her hands

covered her face, which said she was still processing everything that had been said at the table.

Craig took a step to move to her, and then heard the dogs at the back door. Instead, he retreated back to the kitchen and let the dogs into the house.

As if they'd been trained to follow their host, they fell in line behind him, and he walked back to the bedroom and sat down next to Rachel on the bed.

Clyde and Rover sat on the floor at her feet, and she lifted her head. "Damn dogs," she laughed through the tears. "They know how to behave when they need to, and sit there looking up at me with those dark eyes."

"They know you're hurting," he said as he reached for her hand and interlaced their fingers.

"I didn't mean to lose my cool. I'm embarrassed. I guess they didn't expect to see this side of me, huh?"

Craig ran his thumb over her knuckles as he had earlier. "There is no reason to be embarrassed at all. They all know what you're going through. We are all missing your dad."

She lifted her eyes to meet his. "My mood has nothing to do with my dad. I enjoyed listening to them reminisce about him."

Craig tucked a lose strand of her hair behind her ear. "If it wasn't about your dad, what set you off?"

Rachel let out a breath and raised her hand to his cheek. "When they mentioned *your* dad."

CHAPTER 27

C raig focused hard on not tensing at Rachel's mention of his father. He bit down hard until a sharp pain moved through his jaw. He hadn't thought of his father in ten years, why should she?

Rachel pulled her hand from his and bent over to pet the dogs that quietly stared up at her.

Running his teeth over his bottom lip, he took a moment before he spoke. "Why did the mention of my father set you off?" he asked, but realized that his words were strained and angry.

Rachel looked back up at him, her face shadowed by the darkness in the room and the light from the hallway. "I think maybe we need more time."

"More time for what?"

"To work through this."

Craig rubbed the back of his hand over his whiskered chin. The conversation he'd had with Bruce flashed in his mind. "See, this is where I'm not good at this relationship stuff. What are we working through? Are we processing old feelings or starting with new ones?"

"No matter what, it's going to be a little of both, right?"

He nodded slowly. "Right. But it seems as if we keep getting caught up on old feelings." He stood and ran his hand over his hair. "You know, I told Bruce that I wasn't sure if we were starting something new or finishing up the past."

Even in the shadows of the room, he'd seen her eyes go wide. But when she didn't say anything, he wasn't sure where to go from there.

Rachel stood and picked up Rover. Holding her close to her chest, Rachel reached her other hand down to Clyde and rubbed the top of his head.

"I wanted to start something new," Rachel said softly. "But in the moment I didn't realize how much we needed to finish up before we could do that."

"You're right. We were kids then."

"We were. Impressionable kids. Kids that were in love."

He wasn't sure why it ached in his chest when she said the words, but it did. And maybe it was because back then, he'd loved Rachel immensely. Even when he'd gotten married, he had resigned that his true love had been Rachel and he'd let her slip away. Now here she was, and yet, she hadn't exposed all of her secrets to him yet.

"So, what do we do?" he asked running his hand down the sleeve of her shirt, wondering if touching her was the right thing to do.

"The therapist in me says that we should take some time away from each other. We should write down what we feel we need to discuss, then we should move through that list."

Craig reached his hand into her hair. "And what does the woman in you say."

She drew in a long breath and set Rover back down on the ground. "The woman says that she can't stand the thought of anything coming between her and the man she loves."

Now he drew in a breath. "The man she loves?" he asked and

Rachel nodded as she moved to him and placed her hands on his chest. "You love me?"

"I have always loved you," she said as she lifted the hem of his T-shirt and pulled it up over his head.

Well, shit. Inside, he thought the therapist held some merit. They did need to talk. They needed to put the past behind them, mourn her father, and find peace with the rest of the world accepting them. But the man in him, whose body was buzzing from the energy her hands created on his skin, didn't believe in any of that therapist shit. They could just push past it all and start new. That's what they wanted anyway, right?

What was better than to fall right in line with someone he already loved and plan for the future? He knew he loved Rachel, and hadn't she just confessed her love to him?

They could take what they'd built years ago and move forward with it. Hell, he wasn't getting any younger. They could get married and have a family.

As she moved her hands to the button on his pants, he realized his mind was all over the place. God, was he such a man that a woman's touch could render him mindless? Or make him think of weddings and babies?

When she'd run her hands back over his skin, he tried to bring himself into the moment, consciously. She'd said she loved him. What was he going to do with that information?

Craig raised his hands to the buttons on her shirt, and began to release them. Rachel's hands had steadied right on his hip bones, and he wasn't sure he could be nimble enough with the buttons to unfasten them all.

When he'd managed them, he pressed his hand to the swell of her breast, then up her neck, and back into her hair. Her eyes had closed and the light from the hallway illuminated her.

As if the dogs understood what was happening, they both walked out of the room. And, realizing he now had a roommate with access to the upstairs, Craig kicked the door closed.

The room was fully dark now, minus the light that came from under the door. Craig reached to turn on the lamp on the bedside table, but Rachel reached for his hand.

"Leave it off," she whispered and guided his hand back to her chest.

"I want to see you."

"I'm more comfortable in the dark."

"I've seen you naked."

"A long time ago."

He chuckled. "The other day," he reminded her.

Rachel slid her hands under the fabric of his pants and over his ass. Oh, who the hell was he to argue? He'd leave the damn light off, he thought, as her mouth came to his and again rendered him completely senseless.

In the dark, he made love to her, and that was what it was now, he decided as she moved under him. In the beginning it was sex, and it grew into a relationship where there were feelings deeply embedded in the physical touch. Now, there was love.

The shirt she wore lay open, exposing her in the dark, but she'd never actually taken it off. They had a long road ahead of them.

As he pulled her into him, and she pressed a heavy kiss to his chest, he figured he'd give them the benefit of the doubt. Maybe, just maybe, this time they could make it. But only when there were no more secrets.

CHAPTER 28

I n the dark, Rachel climbed from the bed and buttoned her shirt. She slipped on her pants and opened the door.

"Where are you going?" Craig asked, his voice full of sleep.

"I have to let the dogs out, and then I need to head home."

He rolled so that he faced the door. "You can stay. It's really late."

"I didn't plan on staying. Besides, we both have to work tomorrow. And, I didn't bring anything for the dogs."

"I'll get up so I can help you load up."

"You don't have to."

He kicked his legs over the edge of the bed and sat up. "I want to."

Rachel went into the bathroom, turned on the light, and studied herself in the mirror. She thought she should look happier than she did. After all, she'd just had sex with the man she'd pursued since she was a teenager. Then again, she'd hid under him in the dark, again. That wasn't actually exposing herself.

Pulling a hair tie from the front pocket of her jeans, she pulled her hair up into a messy bun and then wiped the dark remnants of eye liner away from under her eyes. She'd see how the next few weeks panned out, and if things progressed, she'd start leaving some personal items for times such as these—and for the dogs too.

The dogs had taken up residence in the dining room. Rover was asleep and curled up against Clyde, who laid there as if it were his job to keep the other dog comfortable.

"C'mon," she said. "Time to go home."

Clyde nudged Rover awake and then took the lead to follow Rachel to the back door.

"I'll come back by for my pans later," she said as she took her coat from the hook at the door.

"I wish you'd stay."

"Next time." She pulled on her coat and moved to him, standing before her in just his unbuttoned jeans. Pressing her hands to his bare chest, he wrapped his hands around hers. "I hope I didn't freak you out earlier."

"When?"

"When I said I loved you. I realize it's been a hot minute, and it probably seems ridiculous, but..."

"I love you too," he cut her off.

Rachel bit down on her lip. "You do?"

"Always have." He leaned in and pressed a kiss to her lips. "Call me when you get home."

"I will."

As she turned, he grabbed her hand. "Stay with me this weekend."

She felt the smile tug at the corners of her mouth. "Here?"

"Yeah. Bring stuff for the dogs and pack a bag."

"Okay."

Picking up Rover, and holding her close, she let herself out the back door and Clyde followed.

. . .

CRAIG WATCHED as they disappeared around the side of the house and then closed and locked the door.

He noticed the flicker of the TV in the basement, and wondered how long it would take to get used to someone living down there.

"You still up?" he called down the stairs.

"Yup," Bruce answered.

Craig walked down the stairs and stood at the bottom. Bruce was watching some Reese Witherspoon romantic comedy. Craig chuckled.

"Best use of your time?" Craig asked.

"Can't get enough of these stupid kinds of movies. Sue me." He turned, muted the TV, and looked up at Craig. "You guys okay?"

"Yeah, I think so. I still don't know what my father had to do with setting her off," he said, but then wondered if Bruce knew. He'd seemed to have all of the answers lately. "What do you know about it?"

"Man, I don't just want to be your bearer of bad news."

"I need the intel."

"Then ask her for it."

Craig leaned up against the wall next to the stairs. "She won't even take her damn shirt all the way off for me. Why would she open up about this yet?"

Bruce shook his head. "What are you doing with her? Seriously? Maybe the two of you should..."

"Get married and have some kids?"

"Wasn't what I was going to say."

"I love her, man. Like you and those stupid movies. I can't get enough."

Bruce stood and walked toward him. "Your dad did his job on you after graduation, and then he went after Coach?"

Craig straightened. "He went after Coach?"

"At some point in his beratement of you, you mentioned that

a real dad would be there for you, like Coach had been. In his drunken stupor, he showed up at Coach's place and threatened to kill him."

"Shit."

"Yeah, and Rachel was right there front and center for it. So was Alex."

Craig ran his hand over his face. "Son-of-a-bitch was never up to any good. Why didn't Alex tell me that?"

"Because you'd told him to go to hell when he tried to talk to you about it. Do you even realize that you didn't talk to any of us between the time we graduated and when Alex's dad died? Let's just say we were all a little surprised to see you at his dad's funeral."

"Why wouldn't I have been there?"

"Because we figured you'd gone off the deep end and wanted nothing to do with any of us. You were married and doing your thing."

There was a heaviness in Craig's chest. "I needed you guys more than you'll ever know."

"You have us. No one holds any ill will. And don't hold it against Alex either. He was just trying to be a friend to Rachel, and to you, so he didn't mention it."

"It's no wonder Hal was put off by my presence."

"You love her?"

Craig looked him square in the eye. "I do."

"She's told you what she's gone through?"

"Not yet."

"I wish you the best, man. To tell you the truth, I can't see you with anyone but her. And if it's really love, you'll work it out."

And that was exactly what Craig wanted to do.

"Now, get out of here. Let me watch Reese in private so I can go to bed. I'm not as lucky as you to have sex and then fall blissfully asleep."

Craig winced. "You heard us?"

"Old house, friend." Bruce chuckled. "But I could have read that from your attire. Nice tat by the way."

Craig looked at his shoulder and admired the tribal design. "I should have it touched up."

"What do you think of Rach's artwork?"

Craig winced. "Let me guess, it's on her arms?"

"Yeah."

"Haven't seen it," he said, again realizing that the only time she'd taken her clothes off completely was that first night in her bedroom, in the pitch darkness.

By the end of the weekend, they'd work their way through it all, he promised himself.

CHAPTER 29

Rachel sat at her desk, her fingers pressed to her eyes. When she heard the tapping on her door, she lifted her head and looked to see Catherine standing there leaned up against the doorjamb, her visitors badge curling up already on her sweater.

"That's the face of a woman who isn't having a spectacular day," Catherine said studying her.

Rachel clasped her hands and lowered them to the desk, her bracelets clanking against the wood as she did so. "You'd know best when I wasn't looking too good."

Catherine stepped into the office and closed the door behind her. "What's going on?"

Rachel scanned a look over her best friend whose eyes had narrowed on her. "You know I can't tell you that."

"And I know you will—if it's something big enough."

And wasn't it, she thought.

"What are you doing here anyway?" Rachel asked pushing her curls away from her face.

"I was dropping off some papers from the district, and I thought we could do dinner. You've been M.I.A. this week, your mom didn't want to talk about it, and that means you have some gossip to share with me."

"You talked to my mom?"

Catherine shrugged. "My mom sent food and I delivered it. So what do you say? Margaritas and nachos?"

"I'll meet you there at six? I have to go take care of the dogs."

Catherine nodded. "I'll see you then." She pointed in Rachel's direction as she opened the door. "And you're going to spill, so don't weasel out. I want details and juicy gossip."

Rachel smiled as Catherine let herself out of the office, and then she looked back at the memo that had crossed her desk and sickness stirred in her belly.

The report which had been submitted by one of the teachers named a student that Rachel had been working closely with. There was a credible concern for the student's life and perhaps violence against others.

RACHEL WALKED into the restaurant and Catherine waved from a table at the bar.

"I already ordered," she said as Rachel pulled out the chair, hung her coat on the back of it, and climbed up into it. "I ordered a pitcher, and if we need a ride home, I have the Uber app downloaded and ready," she teased.

"I think we'll be fine. The last thing I need is a hangover on a Friday," Rachel confirmed.

"True, you already look as if you haven't slept in days," Catherine confronted her as the waitress set their pitcher of margaritas and their glasses on the table.

"I look just fine."

"Liar. Where did you sleep last night?"

"In my bed," she confirmed as she picked up her glass and sipped.

"Okay, what time did you get home?"

Now Rachel narrowed her eyes. "Not that it's any of your business, but I got home at one."

"This morning?"

"Yes."

"Because you were doing what?"

Rachel stirred her straw through her drink. "For your information, I had dinner with Craig, Bruce, Toby, and Ray."

Catherine's eyes widened. "The team?"

"Most of them."

"No Alex?"

"He lives in Boston."

Catherine picked up her drink and took a sip. "That's right. He was my favorite." She smiled. "But seriously, you and Craig?"

"What did my mom tell you?"

"Nothing. That's why I'm asking so many questions. She skirted around anything to do with the team."

"Not that it's any of your business, but we're seeing each other."

Catherine didn't respond right away. She sipped her drink, lifted salt from the rim with her finger, and licked it off. "You made your move quickly."

"When it comes to Craig, I've always moved quickly."

"Yes, you have," Catherine agreed before she took another sip of her drink. "What is it about that guy that gets to you?"

"Fate? True love?"

"And your mom and brother aren't fans of this, are they?"

"I don't care."

"Don't you?"

The waitress returned with a large plate of nachos and set it between them.

Catherine took a chip from under the cheese. "They just don't want you hurt again."

"And my hurting from before wasn't all his fault. Everyone

seems to forget that in this chaos of mourning and renewal for me."

Catherine nodded. "You're right. That's insensitive of us. Especially me."

And that was why the woman had remained her best friend since childhood. There wasn't a secret that Catherine didn't know about Rachel, and vice versa.

"My mother doesn't want to face the fact that Theo's death was the trigger for me. She'd rather put all the blame on Craig and his family."

"They didn't help the situation."

"And now he's in his thirties with a steady job and a home. We all change."

"And aren't you proof of that? I've got your back, Rach. If Craig Turner is what you want, then that's what I want for you."

"Thank you."

"And what does he think about your artwork?" Catherine raised her brows.

Rachel gave her sleeves a tug, and bit back any words she'd rather use for the question. "He doesn't know yet."

"So you haven't slept with him?"

"Let's just say, I've kept it under wraps."

"Geez, Rach, he's going to find out. Don't you think you should be honest with him?"

"I'd like to make sure we're solid before I go telling him that I once left a suicide note that had his name in it."

Catherine winced. "God, I can't believe you were in a place that dark. And here you are, making changes in the lives of people who are now in dark places."

"Well, I don't know about that," Rachel said as she took a nacho from the plate. "Confidential?"

"Confidential," Catherine agreed.

"I have a student, who I thought had made a lot of progress, under watch for suicide and violence."

"Oh, Rachel." Catherine reached for her hand.

"I haven't talked to him since I got the memo."

"You'll do what's right for him. He's in good hands," Catherine said. "Let's lighten this up. How was the sex?"

Rachel let out a laugh. Catherine was always there when Rachel needed a moment of lightness.

CHAPTER 30

G rading was caught up, grades were entered into the computer, and Craig rubbed his eyes as he leaned back in his chair. The desk he had put into the second bedroom had come in handy. As he looked around the room, he thought he'd upgrade and make the room a fully functioning office. He had an opportunity to teach summer classes online, and wouldn't it be nice to have a place to do that from?

As he rested his eyes, he heard his phone buzz on the desk. There was a flutter of hope that resonated in his chest thinking that it might be Rachel.

When he picked up his phone and looked at the ID, he chuckled. Well, it wasn't going to be the voice he'd hoping on the other line, but he had wanted to call Alex anyway. He just hadn't had the guts to do it.

"Hey, bro," he answered the phone.

"What do I hear about you running some halfway house? Bruce is living in your basement?" Alex laughed.

"Gotta keep him off the streets," Craig teased. "What's up?"

"I just found out my mom is going to be having surgery next

month. Nothing big, but I was going to come out. Can I stay in that spare room of yours?"

Craig looked around. He supposed he could hold off on renovating the room for a bit.

"I don't put mints on the pillow," he teased.

"Shit. I heard it was high class." Alex laughed again. "I appreciate it."

Craig leaned his elbows on the desk. "Anything for you, pal. Hey, I had wanted to call you."

"What's up?"

Not that Bruce would be looming in the stairwell, but Craig took the time to shut the door to the bedroom. "I wanted to ask you about Rachel."

"Diaz?"

"Yeah."

"Man, I heard she got her claws back into you."

Craig supposed she had. "We're exploring an adult relationship."

"Wasn't that what you were exploring a decade ago?"

"If only we'd been adults." He ran his hand over her hair. "Bruce let me in on a few things that happened after we graduated."

"And you didn't know about that before?"

"It's been pointed out that I might not have been in a good mindset after my father came into my life."

"Then I'll spare you my opinion on that."

Craig winced. There was some gratefulness in his heart that his father never returned after he'd swooped in and devastated everyone in his presence.

"You spent time with Rachel after that?"

The end of the line grew quiet and Craig heard ice rattle in a glass as if Alex were shaking his drink. "I did. Man, shit, I hate how that sounds."

"It seems as if I'd disappeared from everyone, so I can't hold it against you."

"Listen, your old man made quite a scene. I'm not sure how welcome you would have been if you hadn't disappeared. He marched into Coach's home and accused him of doing things to you that just weren't true. He blamed him for brainwashing you, which included him giving his daughter to you like some kind of prize."

"Shit."

"Yeah. He had learned about Theo too, and dropped some unpleasantries there as well. He threatened to kill them for taking his son from him, which we all knew he'd never made any advancement on that on his own. Mrs. Diaz called the police, they filed a report, no one heard from your dad again."

"Or me."

"He got into your head, man."

"And you stepped in to take care of Rachel."

"And you're going to hold that against me all these years later? I was interested, and she was mad at you. Seemed like a perfect time to do just that, don't you think."

Craig didn't want to think about it at all. "What happened to her that summer? Seriously, I know there's more. She didn't go to school in the fall."

Alex didn't answer right away, but Craig could be patient enough to get his answers.

"You were gone by mid June. And by gone, I mean none of us could find you. I know you moved. Rumor had it you were seeing someone. More rumors had it you were drunk all the time." Hearing that made Craig wince. Someone had been paying attention, even if he'd pushed them all away. "Yeah, I moved in on Rachel. But her mom and Hal didn't want me around any more than they wanted you around at that point."

"So you dated her behind their back?"

"I consoled her, jackass. She was afraid for you. She was afraid for her father. While you were off drunk and doing what you were doing, she was partying quite hard, and yeah, I was there."

"You slept with her?"

"I hate having this conversation over the phone."

"I'm not going to hold it against you."

"Yes you are, and you're not going to believe a word I say until you talk to Rachel and get the truth from her."

Craig ran his hand over the back of his neck. Alex knew him well enough. He was right. He'd made up his mind on what he thought Alex and Rachel had done. "Tell me your side."

"I didn't have sex with her. Don't think I didn't try. But, hell, all she wanted was you back." Alex let out a long breath. "She went down a deep hole, friend. She started drinking, a lot, and then cutting herself."

"That's what Bruce said."

"So then why are you asking me all these questions too."

"I needed to hear the side from the guy who moved in on my turf."

Alex actually chuckled. "Man, I don't know what I was doing except trying to be a friend. In the end, I think my moving in on Rach only made Catherine hate me more."

"Her best friend? What's that about?"

"Seriously? God, she had me twisted up for years, much like Rachel had you twisted up."

"I didn't know that."

"No one did. She didn't much care for us boys back then. She knew someone would hurt Rachel, so every player that came through that house got the stink eye from the bestie."

Now Craig chuckled. He had no idea. "Okay, so finish up the story."

"I know you know the rest."

"They locked her up."

"They got her help," Alex corrected him. "Yeah, she didn't go to school for another year. She got the help she needed after her suicide attempt, which in my opinion was more of a cry for help. But, just in case, she left a note."

The very thought made Craig sick to his stomach.

"That says more than a cry for help to me," Craig said.

"I'm going to go out on a limb and say because of that note, you got the aid you needed from Coach."

"Why's that?"

"Brother, it was all in writing. She couldn't live without you.

CHAPTER 31

The text had come in. Rachel was on her way to his house with the dogs.

Craig had picked up a couple steaks, potatoes, and a salad. And, somewhere in his bellyaching over the past day, he'd convinced Bruce to be somewhere else for the night. Luckily Toby had wanted to talk to him about the job offer, and they were going to make a weekend of it, skiing. That was fine with Craig. Tonight was a pivotal point in the relationship he and Rachel were building.

He knew everything now. All he had to do was get her to admit it to him and they could move forward.

Craig bided his time prepping the steaks and the potatoes. He set out two glasses for wine and let the bottle breathe after he uncorked it. There was soft jazz playing from his Alexa to set the mood.

There was peace in the house, but in his gut, he felt as if he'd swallowed a handful of nails.

He heard the dogs barking as they walked up the side of the house to the back yard. Leaving the steaks on the counter, he moved to the back door to see Rachel open the gate and then bend to take the leashes off the dogs.

Now familiar with the yard, Rover took off and Clyde followed her.

Craig stood in the doorway watching Rachel, and when she turned, her hair moving over her shoulder in a wave of dark silk, she looked up at him and smiled.

He smiled back, hoping that it reached his eyes. He was happy to see her, but the angst building inside of him was making him sick.

"Hi, handsome," she said as she walked toward him, then rose on her toes to press a warm, soft kiss to his lips. Then she looked out over the yard. "They like it here."

"I hope you do too."

She tilted her head to the side as if to study him. "I brought a bag for all of us. We'll see what they think after tonight."

Craig swallowed hard and pulled Rachel through the door and against him harder than he'd meant to, but the need to wrap her in his arms was severe.

"Everything okay?" she asked, her face buried into his chest.

"Yeah. I'm just glad you're here. That's all."

Rachel eased back. "It was a long drive. I'm going to use your restroom and then I'll help with dinner."

Craig released her and she dropped the bag she'd had shouldered by the door and headed down the hall. When he heard the door close, he scrubbed his hands over his face. This was going to need kid gloves, he thought. The goal was to get his information so they could move forward, and not to scare her away and lose her forever.

RACHEL STARED at herself in the mirror for a long moment. Alex had called her that morning while she was at work to tell her that Craig had questions. Everything that she'd gone through since he'd graduated was common knowledge now. All she needed to do was have the courage to show him her scars.

None of what she went through was his fault, and she hoped he knew that.

She took a few moments to check her eyes in the mirror as well. It had been a hard day. The student she'd received the memo on the day before had reached out to her, but now that everyone was on alert, there was so little she could do for him. Help had been dispatched to his house, but he'd run. It weighed heavy on her heart, and yet, here she was revisiting her past so that she could move forward. It all combined and made her want to run too.

Still looking in the mirror, Rachel pulled off the sweatshirt she'd worn, and no doubt would put back on, but for the moment she would expose herself to Craig and see where things went.

Giving her cheeks a pinch and her hair a fluffing with her fingers, she carried the sweatshirt out over her arm and walked back to the kitchen.

His back was turned to her and he was filling wine glasses. Rachel laid her sweatshirt on the back of one of the chairs and wrapped her arms around her as he turned.

With a glass of wine in each hand, Craig scanned his eyes over her and she watched as he fought himself to not appear surprised.

"Alex called me today," she said.

Craig winced. "Did he?"

"I know that all of the missing pieces have been filled in, and you're being very patient with me. So, here I am. Exposing myself to you."

With shaky limbs, Rachel held her arms out to him.

Craig turned and set down the glasses. When he turned back to her, he took her hands, interlaced their fingers, and studied the artwork on her left arm.

Steps in recovery had her tattooing her arm. The oceanic

scene cleverly hid the thirty different scars she had from cutting into her skin, and the one that could have been fatal. Each one hid under a piece of coral or the fin of a fish. To the casual passerby, they'd never see anything than brilliant colors and amazing artwork. But Rachel kept her arm covered up mostly to hide the scars from herself.

Craig ran his hand over her arm and she watched him flinch each time he felt a scar that was raised under his fingertips.

Rachel's heart raced as he traced each fish, each color, each scar, and then placed a kiss in the palm of her hand.

"This is beautiful," he said. "You shouldn't hide it."

"I don't want to see what's under it."

"Your story is under it, sweetheart. Your survival colored in the picture."

"My note said that I wouldn't live without you."

He nodded. "I've heard. And I'm so sorry for the pain I caused you."

She shook her head. "I don't blame you." She might have then, but now she knew better. "I've never had anyone enter my life and tell me that I'm not worthy of the air I breathe. I think having someone whose blood ran through my veins, yet was a stranger, telling me that would set me off. That's what happened to you, and why you turned from everyone. Your father got into your head. He threatened my family. And, he got into my head too."

Rachel watched Craig's Adam's apple bob as he swallowed hard. "I got over it."

"You hid first."

"We'll call it that. But this..." he turned her arm to look at all the colors.

"This was sparked by finding my little brother dead in the bathroom. This was sparked by screaming as I got him down and his limp body falling on top of me. This was his delusion that life was better lived without him." Rachel lifted her hands to Craig's chest. "My letter was me trying to run from loving you, and trying to drown my pain in alcohol. But none of this truly had anything to do with you."

"I'm so sorry that my father..."

She pressed a finger to his lips. "Your father isn't our problem anymore, and you're not your father."

"No, I'm not."

"Then let's start something new."

He gathered her hands in his and pressed kisses to her finger-tips. "Tell me about you and Alex."

Rachel laughed. "He's a lousy kisser," she said and Craig winced. "That's it. Nothing more happened between me and Alex. He was a friend when I needed one, before they sent me away."

"That was all?"

"He knew my heart forever belonged to you."

CHAPTER 32

Rachel exposing herself to Craig had been the turning point in their new relationship, and there was freedom in letting herself be seen by everyone. All of the others on the team knew her secrets, well, most of them had, but now there was full disclosure. There'd been a lot of compliments on her tattoo, and they all appreciated the starfish, which had represented her father.

Routines were started, and it brought a comfort to Rachel she didn't know existed. One weekend they would stay at her house, the next at his. Wednesday nights she made dinner for him and Bruce, but inevitably Toby and Ray showed up as well.

Tuesdays she spent with her mother, and Thursdays had been saved for margaritas and nachos with Catherine.

"I've known you my whole life, and I've never seen you this happy," Catherine said as she licked the last of the salt from her glass rim and finished her margarita.

"I've never been this happy." And that was the truest statement she'd ever made.

It had been six weeks since she laid her father to rest, and admittedly she didn't think her life would take this kind of turn.

Had their promise to her father held her back from happiness, or had she needed this time to appreciate him and Craig? It was the latter, she knew.

She took a sip of her margarita, let it settle on her tongue and pushed it away.

"What's wrong with it?" Catherine asked.

"Just not in the mood for it, I guess. I think over the past few weeks, I've drank too much of Craig's craft beer that his mother and sister bought for him. My palate is toast."

"Too bad for you," Catherine said pulling the discarded margarita over to her and taking a sip. "Tastes fine to me."

"I'm going to have to drive you home tonight."

"That's fine. It's my night with you on your weird little schedule. It gives me five more minutes with you tomorrow too."

"You could always come to Craig's and have dinner with us on Wednesdays," Rachel offered as she took a nacho and bit it in half.

"I don't see the fun in that."

"Who's selling themselves short now? You know Alex will be here next week."

Catherine lifted a brow. "And?"

"I'm just saying."

"Why would you say that to me? What would I care if Alex Burke is in town?"

The smile tugged at Rachel's lips. "Because you have always had a thing for him."

"Bite your tongue."

Rachel laughed as she took a sip from the water the waiter had set on their table when they'd been seated. "You're so full of it. There was no focus on it because it was always about the risqué relationship I was having with Craig. You've done a good job at making it seem as if you're disgusted by him."

Catherine took a long drink from the margarita and then

winced at the freeze it gave her brain. "I think you did serious damage to your brain."

"Nah, my brain is fine now."

"You have issues."

Rachel shrugged. "I'm in love."

"It's gross."

"Come to dinner with me on Wednesday and prove me wrong."

Catherine pressed her palm to her brow and bit down on her lip. "You want me to go with you to Craig's house and eat with the team just so I can prove to you that Alex Burke does nothing for me."

"Yep. I think you owe it to me."

"I think I've done enough for you over the years," Catherine said taking another drink. "But fine. Whatever," her words began to slur.

"Good. Bring a bottle of wine."

CRAIG CRAWLED BACK into bed after having let the dogs outside. His body was cold as he pressed it up against Rachel's, and she squealed.

"We're going to have some rules, Turner. That was just mean," she said as Craig ran his hand down her bare arm.

"The fact that you didn't hit me means you love me too much to be mad forever," he offered, burying his face into her hair.

"I do love you."

"I know." He kissed her shoulder and she reacted with a moan. "Why don't you roll over and show me just how much you love me."

Rachel turned in his arms and then straddled him, pinning his arms over his head. "What do you want?" she asked in a low growl before she bit down on his bottom lip.

"To wake up with you every day of my life, and to crawl back into bed with you after I let the dogs out."

Rachel lifted a brow. "That's what you have to say when I'm in this position?" she laughed. "I was expecting something along the lines of..."

"You'll marry me?"

Rachel eased back, releasing his hands. "What?"

Craig's mouth curled into a smile. He rested his freed hands on her hips and looked up at her. "That's what I want."

Rachel pushed her hair back over her shoulders. "I thought we were playing around."

"We were joking around, but now I'm serious."

Rachel stared down at him and then climbed off of him and off the bed. As she pulled on clothes, Craig wrapped the sheet around him and sat up on the bed.

"What are you doing?" he asked.

"Getting dressed."

"Why?" his voice remained calm and there was some humor to watching her come completely undone.

"I don't know," she stammered as she fought the leg on her pants and then finally got them pulled up. "I didn't expect you to say that."

"But I did."

"Well, knock it off."

"Why?"

As she pulled her shirt on, without having picked up her bra, she turned to him. "Because it's been a little over a month."

"It's been ten freaking years."

"Well, not between who we are now."

"And who are we now?"

She looked at him blankly. "What does that mean?"

"I'm a man in love with a woman. I'm a man whose been in love with that woman for more than ten years, let's be honest. I'm a man with a steady job, his own house, and plenty of room for dogs and kids, and..."

"Don't."

"Don't what?"

"Don't talk like that."

Now he stood up and let the sheet fall. "I love you, Rach. I meant it. Marry me."

She batted her eyes which had gone moist.

Craig lifted a hand to her cheek. "I can replan this. I know this isn't romantic. I don't have a ring, or any clothes on. It was spontaneous and from my heart. But I can wait until you're ready. I'm not going anywhere—ever."

She blinked and the first tear rolled down her cheek. "It wasn't romantic."

"I'll try again."

She shook her head. "No. I don't want you to try again."

He felt the words twist in his gut. He should have considered everything and not have spewed such words like...

"I want to marry you," she said, cutting off his thoughts.

Now it was his turn to blink hard. "You want to marry me?"

Rachel nodded. "I do. And a different proposal would be calculated and cold. Craig Turner, I do want to be your wife. It's been long enough."

CHAPTER 33

It was official, they were engaged. Rachel's hands shook around the casserole dish she held on her lap as they drove to her mother's house on Sunday.

She'd asked Craig not to say anything to anyone before she could tell her mother, and he'd agreed.

Craig hadn't even flinched when she'd asked him to join her at her mother's for dinner on Sunday evening. But now she was nervous for him. Her mother and brother knew about their relationship, and since the day her mother had slapped her, she hadn't brought up his name again. Now, they were pulling up in front of her mother's house, and she was about to announce they were engaged.

Craig put his car in park and reached for her hand. "Are you going to be okay?"

"I'm sick to my stomach," she admitted.

"Would you rather go in on your own?"

Rachel shook her head. "You were always welcome in this house. This is stupid for me to worry that she's going to say anything. Hal is more likely to be a bastard about it, but he'll be fine too." She turned to him. "Why am I so worried?"

"Because you care what they think. You said they spent the past decade blaming me for everything."

"They did, but they didn't even believe it."

"So I saved face for Theo," he said squeezing her hand. "I love you, Rach. No one is ever going to hurt you and I'll never let you hurt. This is a new beginning. Honestly, I'm just sad that I didn't reach out to you years ago, and that your dad wasn't here to see who I became."

Rachel reached her hand up to his cheek. "He knew. He kept tabs on you."

"I have something for you," he said, and Rachel lowered her hand.

"What?"

Craig reached inside his coat, and into the pocket on his shirt. When he pulled his hand out, he held a ring between his fingers.

"I was going to give this to you inside, but maybe I should do it now. Then your mom can see it."

Craig took her hand and slid the diamond solitaire onto her finger.

Rachel looked down at the simple ring and her heart nearly exploded. "Craig..."

"When we set a date, I'll take you and we can get something that fits you more."

"This fits perfectly. I love it. I really love it."

"I was thinking, maybe we should set a date."

Rachel twisted the ring on her finger. "Really?"

"I don't want to wait. I think we waited long enough."

She bit down on her lip. "Name your date," Rachel said smiling.

"August twenty-first. It happens to be a Saturday."

Rachel pressed her fingers to her lips. "You've thought a lot about this."

"Do you know what that date is?"

A giggle escaped her throat. "The date we snuck out and spent the night in your car."

Craig chuckled. "You do remember."

"I could never forget that day. You said you wanted to marry me then."

"That's why I think it would be perfect."

Rachel leaned in and pressed a kiss to his lips. "Mr. Turner, I shall marry you on August twenty-first."

"I can't wait. Do you feel better?"

Rachel laughed as she turned to open the door. "Not in the least. I still feel like I'm going to throw up."

HAL OPENED the door as Craig and Rachel walked toward the house.

"Tell me that's a potato casserole," Hal said as Rachel grew closer.

"Of course. Just for you."

"Mom's in the kitchen." He lifted his eyes to meet Craig's. "I need to push out her trash cans. Craig, will you help me?"

Craig knew this move. He'd pulled it on his brother-in-law himself. "Sure."

Rachel walked into the house as Hal let the door close and they walked around the side of the house.

"Rach is doing okay?" Hal asked.

"I think she's doing amazing."

"Good," Hal said as he opened the side gate. "Mom is worried for her."

"She's well taken care of."

Hal pulled the recycle bin away from the wall and pushed it toward Craig as he retrieved the trash bin. "Tell me about that. How are you taking care of her?"

Craig gave his words some thought as he pushed the can toward the walk and around the house. "First of all, I'd always take care of her. My track record from a decade ago isn't valid now."

"She's come clean about everything?"

"Everything."

"You don't hold that against her?" Hal asked as they set the bins on the street.

"I never could hold that against her. She was impressionable then, and look at her now. Look at what she's done to overcome and to help others."

"She's incredible," Hal agreed.

"She is."

"So, what does the future hold?"

Craig bit down on his bottom lip. "She wanted to tell your mom first, but I've asked her to marry me."

"And she agreed?"

"Save the date for August twenty-first."

Hal laughed. "I guess you're really serious then?"

"I've never been more serious about anything in my life. I love your sister. I have always loved your sister. I will take care of her for the rest of my life."

Hal nodded. "I believe that." He held out his hand to Craig, and he shook it. "I'm sorry that we've been cold to you."

"I understand."

"She told Mom it was because of Theo, and not your leaving. No matter what her note said."

"That's what she told me too. She loved Theo. It still lives with her."

"I can't imagine it would ever go away."

They started back to the house, and Craig thought that went better than he could have imagined. For that, he was grateful.

When they reached the front door, Hal's mother opened it. Hal kissed her on the cheek and passed by her, and then Esther Diaz stepped out of the door and stood in front of Craig.

"It's been a long time since you've come into my home," she said as Craig stood in front of her.

"Yes, ma'am, it has been."

"I spent many years convinced that my daughter's unhappiness was your fault." She wrung her hands together. "I had never considered that her brother had brought that on. I didn't want to consider it."

"I understand."

"She tells me you want to get married."

Craig nodded. "I do. I love her, Mrs. Diaz. I have always loved her."

"I knew that. Everyone knew that."

"I will take good care of her. I promise."

"I know that. Her daddy knew that. You were like one of his sons. Knowing you were hurting back then wore on him."

"I'm sorry."

"No. You never need to be sorry." Esther reached for his hand. "I am honored that you'll be my son. Her father would be proud to have you too."

Craig leaned in and kissed her on the cheek. "That means a lot to me."

CHAPTER 34

Craig held Rachel in his arms as she twisted the diamond ring on her finger and the moonlight cascaded over her skin. He ran his hand over her arm, and she no longer flinched when he skimmed his fingers over the scars that defined a moment in her life.

"Your mom took the news better than I thought," he said softly.

"Because she loves you and Hal respects you."

"But I wasn't top on the list for a very long time."

"We all make mistakes, Craig." She rolled and rested her hands and her chin on his chest. "I think of all the years we lost. We should have been married by and had babies by now."

He ran his hand over her hair. "You think about that?"

"I just figured it wasn't in my plans. But you said when you were married, you didn't want kids."

He pressed a kiss to her head. "I didn't want kids with Colleen." Craig rolled her to her back and lifted himself over her. "But I can only imagine a little girl who looks just like you."

"But do you want to be a father?"

Craig lowered himself and took her mouth. Her arms came

around his neck and her fingers tangled into his hair. "To your children, yes, I want to be a father." There was a moment of enlightenment, but then he saw the worry flash in her eyes. "I promise, I will never be a father like mine. I don't want you to worry about that."

"Craig..."

"I mean it. The few minutes he was in my life didn't count. I had a great mentor in Coach Diaz. I want to be that kind of father."

The moonlight made the tears in her eyes shimmer. A baby with Rachel, the thought swelled in his chest. He couldn't have imagined that day he went to say goodbye to the most important man in his life would be the day his life would begin.

RACHEL DANCED through Craig's kitchen as pots bubbled and aromas filled the air. The knock on the back door was unexpected, and when she looked out the window, Catherine stood on the step with a bottle of wine in her hands.

Rachel pulled open the door and pulled Catherine into a hard hug.

"Are you high?" Catherine laughed as she followed Rachel into the house.

"I'm happy."

"I knocked on the front door but you didn't answer."

Rachel laughed. "Never even heard it."

"It smells amazing in here," Catherine said as she set the wine on the table and shrugged out of her coat, hanging it over the back of one of the kitchen chairs. "What are you making?"

"Bolognese over rigatoni. I have some chicken in the oven, and was just cutting up a salad."

"This is very domestic of you."

Rachel smiled as she pulled two wine glasses from the cupboard. "Does it look good on me?"

Catherine laughed as she sat down at the table. "It does. I see that you don't have your arms covered either."

Rachel turned, leaned against the counter with her hip, a glass in each hand. "Things are different. The scars under all of this paint got me to where I am. It created my defenses, it was brought on by my insecurities. I'm in the position of service to the kids at the school because I have these scars. I have to honor them."

Catherine batted her eyes and Rachel saw that she had teared up.

"Rach, I'm so damn proud of you at this very moment, I could burst."

Rachel moved to the table and set the glasses down. "And I have you to thank for some of this. You never have left my side."

It was then that Catherine grabbed her hand. "What is this?"

"This is my prize in life."

"He asked you to marry him?"

"He did."

Still holding Rachel's hand, Catherine looked up at her. "It hasn't even been two months."

"It's been over ten years in the making. I'm ready."

Catherine drew in a deep breath. "I think you might be." She stood and pulled Rachel to her. "I'm happy for you."

"That means a lot."

Catherine stepped back and picked up the wine. "Do you have something to open this?"

Rachel turned back to the drawers and opened two before she found the corkscrew.

"It's quiet. Where are all the guys? I showed up, and let me tell you I had reservations about it."

"They all went to pick up Alex."

"We could have this bottle downed by the time they get back,"

Catherine joked as she twisted the corkscrew into the top of the bottle and pulled out the cork.

Rachel turned down the heat on the sauce and turned back around as Catherine held out a glass to her.

"What should we drink to?" Rachel asked as she held her glass out to tap against Catherine's.

"You getting your shit together and finally landing the man you've been seducing your entire life."

Rachel laughed as they tapped glasses. Lifting her glass to her lips, the smell caught her first. She followed it through with a large sip, which she immediately turned around and spit out into the sink.

"How long have you had that?"

Catherine looked into her glass. "I just bought it. What's wrong with it?"

"It's rancid."

Catherine sniffed the wine in her glass and then took a sip. "Maybe you've been tasting too much sauce," she laughed. "This is just fine."

Rachel wiped the back of her hand over her lips and laughed. "I guess it's you polishing off that bottle tonight."

"I am not drinking that all by myself," she said as the front door opened and they heard the men walk into the house. "My help has arrived."

"We can have Alex drive you home," Rachel whispered as the four men turned the corner and a moment later all stood in the small kitchen with them.

Craig stepped in and kissed Rachel, and then pulled Catherine into a hug. "She convinced you to come. I'm glad."

"She promised me food that she cooked. How could I not?"

As Craig stepped back, each of the men said hello to her.

Ray shrugged out of his coat. "What do you have to drink?"

Rachel opened the refrigerator. "Beer, and Catherine brought some wine."

Ray took a beer, handed one to Toby, one to Bruce, and offered one to Alex, who shook his head. "I'll have some wine," Alex said and Rachel watched the awkward glances between Catherine and Alex.

Pulling down another glass, she handed it to Catherine to fill and turned back to the sink to rinse out the glass she'd drank from.

Craig's arm came around her waist and he pressed a kiss to her ear.

"Are you okay? Your cheeks are super red," he whispered.

Rachel laughed. "That wine is rancid," she whispered back and pressed a hand to her stomach. "I want to see what he does."

Collectively they turned as Catherine handed Alex the glass filled with wine. He smiled and sipped from the glass, but he certainly didn't give Rachel the satisfaction of the reaction she was looking for.

CHAPTER 35

Bruce carried up his card table from the basement and Ray set up the one that Craig had stashed in his spare bedroom. Alex and Toby collected chairs and set the around the tables as Catherine helped Craig and Rachel carry out plates and bowls of food.

The thunderous conversations that crossed over one another filled a place in Rachel's heart that had been empty for a very long time. With Alex and Catherine there, everything seemed to be right.

She'd grown up with this chaos at her table. These same faces, now aged slightly and the voices deepened. They razzed one another and complimented in the next breath.

Alex looked tired, but then Rachel had caught sight of herself in the mirror before dinner too. Maybe life was wearing on them all.

Toby always looked out of place, but wasn't. He and Bruce now had their own inside conversations about work that no one else understood. Ray and Craig had reminisced something about high school and laughed, then Craig reached for Rachel's hand and interlaced their fingers on top of the table.

Alex, now on his third glass of wine from Catherine's bottle, tipped it toward Rachel. "That is one hell of a tat, Rach," he said, his words slightly slurring.

She looked down at her arm, now more appreciative of the artwork. "Thanks. It was time to show it off," she said, and Craig lifted her hand to his lips and kissed her fingers. And that was when Ray came out of his seat, pulled her hand from Craig's and examined her finger.

Her hand still in his, he looked at his watch. "Three hours and forty-five minutes."

Alex laughed. "What is three hours and forty-five minutes?"

"Since I got here, climbed in Craig's car, picked you up at the airport, and we ate dinner."

"Okay," Alex topped off Catherine's drink and finished the bottle of wine. "And?"

"And neither of them said a word about being engaged?" He shifted his glance between Craig and Rachel as the room grew quiet.

Craig pulled Rachel's hand back from Ray's grasp and planted a long, warm kiss to her lips. "She said yes. So, hey guys," he said without looking away from her. "We're getting married."

Each of the men who Craig called brother, stood from their seats to hug her and slap him on the back. The basketball star and the coach's daughter—finally, they rallied. Catherine sat at the end of the table and laughed, and Rachel appreciated her being there.

There was no other group of people she'd rather celebrate her future with, her mother and brother excluded, she thought.

Bruce left the room and came back with an armful of craft beers, and Rachel laughed knowing he hadn't even made a dent in what Craig had in the refrigerator.

He handed one to everyone, including Catherine. When he handed one to Rachel, she looked at the label and shook her head.

"I'll trade you," Toby said, looking at his label.

"I just think I'll pass. I ate too much before you all got here. I had to test it," she joked.

Bruce passed around the bottle opened and they all lifted their bottles in celebration, Rachel lifting her water glass.

"To the two of you," Bruce began. "God damn you took forever to get to this point. It's about freaking time," he toasted.

There seriously couldn't have been a better toast for the celebration, Rachel thought.

As the bottles clinked, Clyde brushed up against her leg. "I'll be back," she dismissed herself and walked the dogs to the back door, and out into the yard, standing in the coolness of the night for a moment, which felt good against her warm skin.

The door opened to her back and Alex joined her. "What are their names?" he asked as the dogs ran through the yard in the dark.

"The little one is Rover, and she thinks she's as big as Clyde. But he doesn't correct her."

"Rover is a she, huh?"

"Biggest dog you'll ever know," she joked. "I'm glad you're here," she said looking up at him.

"I just wanted to tell you that I'm proud of you." He took her hand and held it in his. "When Craig began asking me questions, well, I just didn't know what to do with that. I guess I always figured he knew."

"It's okay. Everything needed to be said so we could get to this point."

"I'm torn with guilt over having moved into his territory, and being glad that I did. I hope I was able to diffuse some of the hate spewed toward him. He's not his father."

"He's not. And for what it's worth, it made Catherine very jealous."

Alex looked toward the door and back at Rachel. "She never liked me. I don't think she was jealous."

"She was jealous."

"I love you, friend. I'm glad you're happy."

Rachel lifted on her toes and placed a kiss on Alex's cheek. "I love you too, friend," she repeated the sentiment.

"Even if I'm a lousy kisser?"

She felt the heat rise in her cheeks. "Who told you that?"

"Craig did, of course. Anything to diss me." He gave her hand another squeeze. "I never could compete with him."

Alex smiled as he turned and walked back into the house.

No, she thought, he never could have competed with the love she had for Craig.

A small breeze blew through the yard, and she should have been frozen, but even standing outside, she wasn't cold. In fact, she'd been burning up surrounded by all of their friends.

She pressed a hand to her forehead and then to her stomach. Catherine and Alex were going to be sick in the morning, after drinking that rancid wine, she thought.

The thought humored her as she called for the dogs. Catherine vowed that she hated Alex Burke, but she had no reasoning to back up her claim. And Alex bought into that. But Rachel clearly remembered how jealous she'd become when Alex had moved in on Rachel. Now she wondered how much of that was an act.

It would be interesting to see if anything transpired between Catherine and Alex while he was in town.

CHAPTER 36

The house was reminiscent of their college days, Craig thought as he stumbled to the kitchen before dawn on Thursday morning to start the coffee maker.

Bruce was tucked into his own space in the basement, and Toby was asleep on Bruce's couch. Alex had given up the spare bedroom to Catherine, who after two more beers, agreed with Rachel that the wine might have been rancid.

Alex slept in one of Craig's recliners and Ray had taken over the couch. It was going to be a shitty way to start a morning, but as he filled the coffee maker with grounds, Craig smiled. They were all together, and that warmed his heart.

He'd heard the bedroom door open and the bathroom door quickly close. The dogs appeared at his feet, and he opened the back door and let them out before moving back to the coffee maker.

Craig added water to the machine when he sensed someone behind him. When he turned, Catherine was leaned up against the doorjamb, her hair messed from sleep, still in her clothes.

"Happy Thursday," he chirped and she groaned.

"I haven't done this in forever," she said holding her hand to her stomach. "Is that your only bathroom?"

"Bruce has one downstairs."

"I'm not going down there," she said pulling a chair back from the table and sitting down. "It's going to be a long day."

"But we had some fun, huh?"

She chuckled. "Yeah, we did. So what did her mom say when you told her you were getting married?"

Craig turned and leaned his hip on the counter. "I got a small shake down from both her and Hal, but I really think the coach vouched for me even now. I'm not my father. I've only ever loved Rachel, even when I was married, and that was some of the problem there too, I'd assume. I have their blessing now."

"I didn't see it coming this soon," Catherine admitted.

"I think it took too long," Craig admitted as he heard the bathroom door open and Rachel stumbled into the kitchen. He studied her for a moment. Dark circles darkened her eyes, and her hair clung to her wet face.

Before he could move to her, Catherine jumped up. "Are you okay? You look worse than I feel."

"I'm telling you, you're going to look like this," Rachel said. "That wine was bad."

"Great. I drank half that bottle of wine and three beers. My stomach is already sloshing. We should take a sick day."

Rachel shook her head. "I can't. I have a meeting about that student," she bit down on her lip and Catherine nodded. "I'd better get my stuff together and get home to get ready."

Now Craig moved to her. "You can shower here. Leave the dogs for the day. Alex will be here for a while. Bruce will be around."

"It'll be okay. The drive home will clear the fog from my brain." Rachel turned back to the bedroom and closed the door.

Craig exchanged glances with Catherine. "What's the meeting about the student?" Craig asked.

Catherine looked down the hall at the closed door and back up at him. "She said it's confidential."

He winced. "But you know?"

"I know."

"One of her students is having troubles?"

"You could say that."

"And she's helping them?"

Now Catherine smiled. "That's what she does."

Craig nodded as Toby walked into the kitchen. Rachel helped others, it was what she did. And in that moment, pride swelled in his chest. She was made to help people.

RACHEL SAT at her desk wiping her eyes with a tissue when Catherine tapped on her office door.

She sniffed back her tears and looked up at her friend who looked more put together than Rachel felt, and wasn't she hung over?

"Hey, what's wrong?" Catherine walked in and shut the door.

"Long morning. What are you doing here?"

"Checking on you under the veil of district paperwork delivery. Waiting for the principal's signature, but he's in a meeting. But seriously, what's wrong?" she asked taking a seat in front of Rachel's desk.

"They put him in juvenile detention," she whispered as if the walls would pass on their secret.

"The student that they warned you about?"

Rachel nodded. "He threatened his family." She wiped at the tears again. "I'm sick. I'm just sick."

"Rach, you do your best. This has nothing to do with you."

She lifted her eyes to meet Catherine's. "But deep inside, I need to know that I can help."

"You did."

"Did I?" She threw the tissue in the trash and pulled out another. "He asked for me, and my hands are tied. I can't go running to his aid. Not outside of school."

"He asked for you?"

"Yes."

"So you got through to him?"

"If I had, he wouldn't have threatened his family. What he needs is good care. But I don't know that he's going to get what he needs in juvenile detention."

"You've already started a letter to them, haven't you?"

Rachel chuckled through her tears. "Yes. I'm asking that the courts find him help. And soon."

"I'm so sorry, Rach. I wish there was something I could do to comfort you."

"I'm comforted by the fact that you look like shit, even dressed up with your hair curled," she teased.

"I think you're right. That wine was bad. My stomach aches," Catherine admitted.

"I've thrown up three times today," Rachel whispered again.

"You only had one drink. Hell, you spit that out."

"You're doomed," she teased, and took a breath. "Thank you. I needed a laugh."

Catherine studied her before standing and walking to the door. "It's Thursday night. Margaritas and nachos?"

The very mention of it made Rachel cringe. "I just can't do it tonight."

"Are you going to Craig's?"

She shook her head. "No. Thursdays are for margaritas and nachos," she laughed. "Maybe we could just get a bag of salad and eat it in my kitchen."

"I'll bring it with me and I'll be at your house at six," Catherine agreed.

Catherine gave Rachel a wave and let herself out of the office.

When she was alone, Rachel rested her head on her arms atop her desk.

Her stomach knotted and her heart ached when she thought of the student she'd worked with all year. It didn't help that there were so many similarities between him and Theo, but Theo never lashed out violently to others.

She lifted her head and looked at the file on her desk. Miguel White's photo stared back at her. The letter sat on her computer screen waiting for her final touches.

He needed help. This was her job, the one she'd poured her heart and soul into. She went back to the letter, begging for the state to help the troubled young man, and save his life.

CHAPTER 37

Craig walked into the sushi restaurant where Alex sat at a table near the door.

"I'm glad you could make it," Alex said as he stood to shake Craig's hand. "I wasn't sure if I'd catch you on your lunch break."

"How's your mom?" Craig asked as he sat down across from Alex.

"She's nervous. Sarah is staying with her, which seems to keep her calmer than if I were around all the time. When I'm there, she wants to worry over me. I'll be at the hospital when she's in surgery and recovery. She can't worry over me there."

"Give her my best," Craig said.

"I will." Alex looked at the order form and then handed it to Craig. "Congrats on your engagement, by the way. Should have happened years ago."

"Thanks. Will you be able to be out here in August? I want all of you to stand with me."

Alex picked up his glass of water and took a sip. "I've been thinking about that. I think it's time I come home."

Craig marked the order form and set it to the side. "You're ready to leave the East Coast?"

"Yeah. It's time to start over, here. So I wanted to talk to you about it. I know it's bad timing, since Bruce just moved in, but would you consider renting me the spare room until I get situated? I can ask Ray too. I know this isn't convenient."

"Dude, the room is yours. Rach and I are going to have to decide where to live."

"What did your mom and sister say?" Alex asked as he handed the order form to the waitress that stopped by their table.

"We called them after we left the Diaz's house on Sunday. I'd say Mom was a bit surprised. Certainly not disappointed, but surprised."

"I think we're all surprised. I knew something was going to happen when she talked to you at the funeral. But, I'll admit, this isn't what I thought it would be."

Craig picked up the water glass in front of him and sipped. "I'm not getting any younger. I don't want to wait any more. She's the only one I've ever loved. With her, marriage and family feels right."

"I'm happy for you, man. I really am. And, if you move into her house, I could buy yours."

Craig laughed. "You always were quick on your feet."

RACHEL SAT on the corner of her couch with Rover in her lap, and Clyde curled up on her feet. The moment she'd gotten home from work, she'd pulled on a pair of flannel lounge pants and an oversized sweatshirt. She'd tied up her hair and scrubbed off her smeared makeup.

The day had dragged her down, and all she wanted was to cuddle with her dogs and forget about it.

Catherine had already texted and said she was on her way with that salad Rachel had requested.

She'd forever be grateful for her best friend.

Clyde snored at her feet, and Rachel closed her eyes, which stung from the tears she'd cried all day. Then she heard the car in her driveway.

Moving the dogs, she stood up, walked to the door, and opened it as Catherine pulled bags from her backseat. She laughed when she started toward the door with three bags.

"I just wanted a salad," Rachel said as Catherine walked toward her. "What did you bring?"

Catherine handed her one of the bags as she walked through the door. "You had a hard day. Pints of ice cream were in order. I didn't bring wine, not after the hangover I had from last night."

Rachel laughed. "I think you're lucky that's all you got." She shut the door and followed Catherine to the kitchen as the dogs moved from the couch and fell in step.

Rachel pulled a bowl from the cupboard, two plates, and forks as Catherine set out four different pints of ice cream.

"Did you have a bad day too?" Rachel laughed as she set the plates on the table and turned back to open the bag of salad mix into the bowl.

"A hung-over day. I just think it's a night for indulgence."

Catherine put the ice cream in the freezer as Rachel set the bowl of salad mix on the table and picked up the last bag that Catherine had carried in.

She reached her hand into it, noticing there was still a box in the bag. Slowly, Rachel pulled out the box and scanned a long look over the pregnancy test she held in her hand.

Raising her eyes toward Catherine, she watched as she slowly closed the freezer door, her lips tucked between her teeth.

"Is this why we're going to need all that ice cream?" Rachel asked.

"Maybe."

"Catherine, I didn't know. I mean, who? I mean, no, really?"

Catherine moved to her, wrapping her hands around Rachel's hand that held tight to the box.

"Rach, it's not for me."

"Oh." She swallowed hard. "So why did you buy this?"

"The wine wasn't rancid and that margarita last week was just fine too."

"You bought this for me because alcohol tastes funny to me?"

"I bought it because I think you and Craig might be moving things a long even faster than you think you are."

Her hand began to shake as she looked at the box.

"This didn't cross my mind."

Catherine nodded. "If it's negative, then I'm out a few bucks."

"If it's positive?"

Now Catherine laughed. "Honey, if its positive you and Craig get to start that fairy tale life even sooner."

"You think I'm pregnant?"

"I do. I know you very well. The past few weeks you're just a little different, and I know it's not all about this student."

"It could be negative."

"It could be."

Rachel let out a long breath to steady herself. "Well, I guess there is only one way find out, right?"

"I'll be right here for you."

Rachel nodded. "What do I want this to say?"

Catherine kissed her on the cheek. "Does it matter?"

"No, you're right, it doesn't matter. If I'm not pregnant, life is normal. If I am," the tears started, "then I guess I'm going to be a mother."

"A mother to a baby with a man you've loved since you were a kid."

"Wow."

"Wow."

CHAPTER 38

Rachel walked back into the kitchen, the pregnancy stick still in her hand. Catherine looked up at her, Rover sitting in her lap enjoying the attention Catherine had been giving her.

"Well?"

Rachel looked down at the stick. "At least these new ones spell it out. Remember in high school when you took one of these and we couldn't figure out what it said."

"Seriously? You bring that up?"

"It's the only time I'd even seen one."

"You're killing me," Catherine said. "For the first time in our lives, I can't read you."

"I had wanted to ask you if you'd be my maid-of-honor."

Catherine sat silent for a moment. "Did you actually pee on that damn stick?"

"Well?"

"Well? You want an answer now?"

"Yeah."

"Of course I'll be your maid-of-honor, you know that."

Rachel smiled and turned to the refrigerator. Pulling open the freezer door, she pulled out the mint chocolate chip pint. Taking out two more spoons from the drawer, she sat down next to Catherine, who watched her closely.

She handed Catherine a spoon and opened the pint. "One thing is for damn sure, I'm not going to get fat all by myself."

Catherine studied her. "It's positive?"

"It's positive," Rachel choked out the words and then the tears began, but they were happy tears. She couldn't believe that Catherine had deciphered the little changes in her when even she hadn't noticed them.

Rachel watched as her best friend wiped her moist eyes. "I told you the wine was fine," she said and they laughed.

"I'm going to take a sick day tomorrow. Will you drive me over to Craig's?"

THERE WAS something about the sound of sneakers on a wooden floor that excited Craig even after so many years. Bruce shouted at the TV and Alex shook his head.

Maybe it wasn't the basketball game on the TV at all, but the brotherhood that had been reclaimed. Now, here they sat, grown men and roommates again.

Beyond the noise of the game, Craig heard the barking of dogs outside his window. He stood and walked to the front window and looked out to see Catherine's car out front, and she, Rachel, and the dogs climbing out.

He pulled open the front door as the dogs hurried up the front walk. He knelt down and gave each of them head rubs, excited to see them when he thought he wouldn't for another day.

Catherine held up a plastic grocery bag. "I have ice cream," she announced.

"Good. We could use something to go with our unhealthy diet

of beer and chips while watching the game," Craig laughed and noticed from the corner of his eye that Alex had stood from his seat when Catherine walked into the house.

Craig watched as Rachel walked up the front walk. "Were you missing me?" he asked.

The glow of the porch light lit up her smile, but then he noticed her hair and her lounge pants. Something didn't look quite right.

He stepped outside, pulling the door behind him. "Are you okay?"

Rachel looked up at him, taking his hand as he offered it. "I had a really long day."

"I didn't expect you. Is that all that's wrong?"

She let out a long breath. "They locked up one of my students."

"Oh."

"I can't really discuss it, but it got to me."

Craig reached a hand out to caress her cheek. "I'm glad you're here. And I'm sure Alex will be more than happy that you brought Catherine." Rachel chuckled and he drew her in. "Are you staying?"

"I'm going to take a sick day tomorrow, so yeah. I'd like to stay."

"Are you sick?"

She shook her head. "No."

"Alex wants to buy my house," he said and she eased back to look at him.

"He's coming back for good?"

"He wants to. But he figured we'd be better living at your place so he could buy this place."

"We should talk about that. Moving in together, that is."

"When you're ready." Craig lifted her fingers to his lips and kissed them.

"I'm ready."

"Let's go inside. We'll make decisions tomorrow." Craig took her hand to walk back into the house, but she tugged him back.

"I think we need to discuss it now."

Craig turned back to her and studied her in the shadows. "Sweetheart, you're starting to scare me. Are you sure you're okay?"

Rachel put her hand into the pocket of her jacket and pulled something out. "The wine wasn't rancid."

He chuckled again. "The wine last night? Alex and Catherine thought it was okay."

"But she knew I wasn't okay. She bought this for me."

Rachel handed him the item in her hand and he took it. He studied it for a long moment and then moved closer to the porch light.

It took him a moment to realize he was holding a pregnancy test and the small window spelled out the word PREGNANT.

His breath came more rapidly as he looked at it. "Catherine bought this?"

"Yes."

"For you?"

"Yes."

"This is you? Us?" He turned to her. "We're..."

She was crying now. "Yes."

Craig moved back to her and took her hands. "We're expecting a baby?"

She only nodded.

"I didn't expect this."

Rachel batted her eyes. "We talked about it, but I didn't know. I didn't know I was already pregnant. Are you angry? Does this change things? I wasn't ready for this. I didn't..."

Craig cupped her face and pressed his lips to hers. "We're having a baby."

Rachel nodded.

"Rachel Diaz and Craig Turner are having a baby."

She nodded again, but a small laugh escaped her. "Are you mad?"

"How could I ever be mad?" He kissed her again. "I love you, Rach. God, this is the greatest thing I've ever heard."

"Really?"

"All I've ever wanted was to marry you and have a family. Here we are." He laughed harder. "Oh, we broke that promise to your dad hard, didn't we?"

She laughed as she leaned in against him. "I think he'd have gotten over it."

Craig slid his hands inside her jacket and rested them on her stomach. "A baby. Sweetheart, this is the best thing that's ever happened to me in my life. I promise you both, I'll be the best father any child ever had."

CHAPTER 39

Craig walked through the front door holding Rachel's hand and three sets of eyes lifted to watch them walk in.

Without a word they walked to the kitchen and the others followed.

"Everything okay?" Alex asked as they all filtered into the tiny kitchen and Craig pulled two bottles of water from the refrigerator.

"Everything is perfect," he said exchanging glances with Catherine, who was grinning.

Alex shifted a look between them and then put his arm around Catherine. "Something's up."

"Of course something's up," she said into Alex's ear, and Craig wondered if she'd meant to stir his friend up, because he'd seen the intimate move cause a flash of something in Alex's eyes.

"I'm taking my fiancée to bed," Craig said smiling at their friends and wrapping his arm around Rachel as they began to walk out of the room. Then, he stopped, pulled the test out of his pocket and threw it toward Alex. "Be careful. There's something in the water," he said as they continued to walk.

From behind him he heard the mumbling, and then, Alex's voice rose above the laughter in the kitchen. "You knocked her up?"

When Rachel laughed, he knew everything was right in the world. He had a house full of friends, the woman of his dreams in his arms, and a baby on the way. A few weeks earlier everything had seemed bleak, and now he was walking on clouds. Never in a million years could he have guessed that Rachel's news, unplanned, would have made him so happy.

Craig locked the bedroom door, then turned and pulled Rachel into his arms.

"Are you happy?" he asked her, pulling the tie from her hair and watching the curls fall around her shoulders.

"I haven't absorbed all of this yet. I was scared."

"Why would you be scared?"

"I didn't plan this. I'm not trapping you, or..."

"Whoa," he silenced her with a kiss. "Never would I think you'd do that."

"I guess I forgot to take my pills. I don't even know. Since dad got sick everything has just..." She stopped talking and pressed her cheek to his chest. "I'm happy, Craig. I really am."

He wasn't sure how to take that, but he wouldn't question it. "Are you just worked up over that student?"

"Maybe. And then Catherine buying that test, that threw me for a loop."

Craig eased her back so he could look at her. "I think you would have figured it out by next week," he said smiling down at her. "She just knows you that well. And now that I know, I can imagine the little things that set her off to assume."

"I had no idea."

"Then we owe Catherine a great deal of gratitude." He brushed her hair back over her shoulders. "Are you going to make a doctor's appointment?"

"I'll see if I can get in tomorrow."

"Good." Craig pressed a hand to her stomach and took a breath. "I can't wait for this. I've never been so excited about anything in my life."

"I'm glad to hear you say that. I suppose we'd better start talking about plans. Settling in together and moving up the wedding."

"Why do we have to move it up?"

Rachel looked up at him and smiled. "Because I'll be five months pregnant."

"So?"

She wrapped her arms around him. "My dad's birthday is at the end of May. Let's get married on that day."

"You don't think people will think that's weird?"

She shook her head. "Not the people that will be there. I don't need big, Craig. I need us and those who have been with us on this journey. To tell you the truth, all I need is you and our baby."

"Our baby. I love the sound of that."

Rachel let out a breath. "Good. I'm starting to get excited now. I can't believe you knocked me up."

Craig let out a laugh as he gathered her up in his arms and set her on the bed. "Talk about a horrible team captain. Running off with the coach's daughter and knocking her up."

Rachel shook her head and giggled beneath him. "He'd be proud of you—of us."

"I think he would be."

RACHEL SAT on the cold table in her doctor's office, the robe she wore open in the back and the paper cover crinkled in her hand.

She tensed when the door opened. "Rachel, congratulations."

She let out a small sigh. "Thank you."

"How do we feel about this pregnancy?"

"I feel like I'm still in shock."

"You weren't expecting it?"

Rachel shook her head. "Not yet. We just got engaged."

"Congratulations on that too," the doctor said as she made a note of the engagement. "Let's get some measurements and see how you're doing."

The doctor eased the bed back and Rachel realized her hands shook. She listened to the doctor's instructions as to what she was doing, and what the machine was for. Then she inserted a wand into Rachel and the screen lit up.

"There we are," she said as a small bubble came into view.

"That's the baby?"

"Yeah, what do you think?"

Rachel laughed. "I think I'm lucky to even see it. It's tiny."

"Well, it appears you're only about two weeks in. Most women don't even know they're pregnant at this stage. You must have had some early signs."

"I have a best friend who knows me better than I know myself," she said laughing again.

"We'll print this out and you can show it to the daddy. And he's welcome to come with you to your appointments. It's good to share this time with him too."

Rachel nodded as the doctor pushed a few buttons and a moment later handed her the image. Tears welled in Rachel's eyes as she looked at the picture of the bubble that would someday be her baby—hers and Craig's. That baby was fate, she knew. This was always meant to be.

CHAPTER 40

The picture of the baby was taped to the front of the refrigerator in Rachel's house. She smiled as Craig placed a kiss on his fingers and then pressed it to the picture when he opened the door for milk.

He'd moved into her house the following weekend after she'd told him about the baby. And to Rachel, it had been absolute bliss for the following six weeks, minus any morning sickness.

After she'd gone to the doctor to confirm her pregnancy, her body had decided to give her the full experience. She'd been sick two or three times a day since then. All she could hope was that after two months it would go away, but so far, it had stuck around.

"Alex wants to have a barbecue in his backyard this weekend," Craig said as he stirred the milk into his coffee. "I told him I was sure we could be there, but I'd check with you since graduation was on Friday morning and you were expected there."

Rachel let out a groan. What was she going to do if she had to get sick right in the middle of graduation?

"We can make it."

Craig had worked out a rental agreement with Alex and

Bruce, until he decided exactly what he wanted to do with the house. There was nothing but time, he'd told them, but she knew he had a sentimental attachment to the house in North Denver, and she'd have to consider that maybe that's where he'd want to land when the baby was born. But for now, he seemed content sharing her bed in the house where she and her dogs once were the only occupants.

Craig turned and leaned against the counter. "You don't look well. Maybe you should call in."

Rachel laughed. "Billions of women have had babies and gone to work. I'm fine." She ran her hand over her flat stomach. "She just doesn't like me."

"She? Is that this week's term? Last week it was he. The week before it was it."

"Keeping it real, Turner."

"I can't wait to meet her," he smiled as he moved to her. Leaning down, he kissed Rachel on the lips and pressed his hand to her stomach. "I didn't realize I could love someone I've never met this much."

Didn't she know it?

Twenty minutes after Craig had left, Rachel carried her bag out to the car and climbed inside. She had to sit for a moment and take a collection of how she was feeling. There had been more than one occasion where she'd had to get out of the car, run back in the house, and get sick.

THE SCHOOL WAS BUZZING, as it often did during spring. The halls were sans seniors who would graduate in the morning, and didn't it always humor her that the juniors instantly got an ego?

There were cookies in the office, next to the coffee pot, and the copy machine. They called to her, and she decided to take a couple and she'd pay for it later. This was supposed to be a thrilling time where she got to eat everything she wanted and didn't have to worry about it.

As she turned to walk into her office, she spotted the wife of their principal walking toward her. She too was in county administration with Catherine, and when Rachel saw the smile on her face, she knew she'd spoken to her.

"Ms. Diaz, you have a glow about you," she said as she pulled her in for a hug.

"Do I?"

Corinne Thompson, dressed in a blue suit which accentuated her dark eyes, smiled wide. "Catherine says you're getting married and expecting a baby. There is no better reason to glow than that, I say."

"I appreciate it." She placed her hands on her stomach. "We're just getting started. Eight weeks."

"At least you won't be huge in the summer. I had our son mid-July. That was tough, but worth it."

"I can't wait to meet her," she said and then added, "or him."

"Babies are such gifts. I'm very happy for you."

"Thank you," Rachel said as she grinned back at the woman.

"We'll see you at graduation tomorrow?"

"Yes, I'll be there."

Rachel watched as the woman moved to another office, then she walked into her own office and closed the door so that no one could see her eat the cookies she'd taken.

As she sat down at her desk, her cell phone rang and her mother's smiling face came up on the screen.

"Hello, Mama."

"How are you feeling?" her mother asked, her voice as chipper as a bird's song.

"It's moment to moment," Rachel said breaking off a piece of one of the cookies.

"I was like that with you. I think it's a girl. I was sick, then I wasn't, then I was," she continued. "With Hal and Theo, nothing."

Rachel laughed as her mother went on and talked about the neighbors and her dinner with a friend.

It was hard to believe that Rachel had been nervous telling her mother about her pregnancy. She'd taken to the news of her marrying Craig Turner better than Rachel had thought, but the news of the baby, that had sent her mother over the moon.

They missed her father, everyone did, but the new beginnings happening all around her seemed to have taken the sting out of it a bit.

She took the bite of the cookie and tried to enjoy it, but the wave of sickness was wavering in her belly again.

"C'mon, little one. Let me have a moment here," she said with her hands over her stomach.

She jumped when her office door burst open and the principal hurried in. "We're having an emergency meeting in the conference room now."

"What's going on?" Rachel pushed back from her desk and took just a moment to steady herself.

"Miguel White escaped from the juvenile detention center. We're on alert."

CHAPTER 41

There were already police cars in the parking lot, Rachel noticed when she looked out the window.

"We're on lock in," the principal said wiping the back of his hand over his brow. "Right now we're on secure alert. We're to keep everyone in the school, and no one comes in. This is a precaution, but due to his case file, they want to keep the campus secure."

Rachel stepped into the room further. "Did his caseworker at the detention center say anything about his possible motive?"

"Just that White didn't feel as if he was being listened to. He was being medicated for schizophrenia, but there is reason to believe that he wasn't taking his medication."

Rachel gripped the back of the closest chair to steady herself from another wave of sickness.

"Ms. Diaz, they'll be coming to talk to you. You know him best."

Rachel nodded and listened to the protocol that was being set in place.

∽

CRAIG SAT in his classroom and watching the thirty people taking their final exam. End of semester not only brought great joy, but great tension.

There was the eighteen-year-old in the front row chewing on her pencil and he wondered if she was going to chew right through it. The mother of four, who was looking to educate herself before going back into the workforce, going back and forth from her notes to the test. The guy who had his skateboard upside down under his feet had fallen asleep. And then there was the young man in the back of the room who had breezed through the test in fifteen minutes, but sat with his arms crossed just watching everyone else finish.

When his phone lit up on his desk, which he'd silenced the tone and the buzz, he looked down to see a text from Rachel.

Giving the room another scan, he slid his finger over the screen to read the message.

The school is in secure mode. We are locked in. Student escaped detention center. This is just precaution. Just wanted you to know. And, we love you.

Craig let out a quiet breath. It wasn't the first time they'd been on lockdown, and sadly it was all common place, but it still always got his heart going. But as he read it again, he couldn't help but smile at her newest sign off. We love you.

Trying not to draw attention to himself, he returned her text.

Be careful. Keep me updated. I love you both.

RACHEL PULLED up all of her electronic files on Miguel White on her computer, and retrieved the physical file as well. She hoped he would just turn himself in and not get hurt, or hurt anyone. He was a good kid with a great dose of problems.

The sickness that had been swimming in her stomach continued, and Rachel reached for her bottle of water, taking a sip and hoped that it would ease.

An hour later when a representative from the police department walked into her office, Rachel turned over everything she had on Miguel White, and explained what she knew about him.

It wasn't long after that that those in the office were told that he'd been found at his home and they had lifted the secure status on the school.

The day, though still fueled with a buzz of anxiety, went back to planning mode for graduation.

BEFORE LUNCH, Rachel checked her phone and realized she'd been so preoccupied, she hadn't noticed the influx of text messages that had poured in.

Her mother had texted. *Are you safe? The news says you're locked down.*

Her brother's text read nearly the same.

Catherine had texted shortly after they had called the original meeting. *That boy you've worked with escaped his detention center. I hear they sent security your way. Stay safe, my friend. Don't forget, you help people all the time, and some of them just need more help than one person can give. I love ya!*

Rachel chuckled when she'd read that one. Wasn't it Catherine that always told her how proud she was of her trying to save the world, but then reminding her that it was a bigger job and she couldn't do it alone?

Craig had texted again. *I'm on summer vacation. Well, for a week before summer session planning starts. Are you doing okay?*

Rachel responded to his text first. *They've lifted the lockdown. He was found at his parents' house.*

She could hear the sounds of students heading through the halls to lunch, and the cars moved through the parking lot outside her window.

She looked back at her phone as the next text came through. *I love you. I'll meet you at home.*

Rachel realized that she was smiling, and it happened every time he texted or called. She was glad that she'd talked to him at the funeral and things had turned out the way they had. Though, never could Rachel have imagined that between February and the end of May, her life could completely change.

She pressed her hands to her belly. "He loves us, sweetheart," she whispered just as she heard the screams from the hallway and saw the flash that blew out the windows of the main office, just outside her open door.

Her first instinct was to run to the door and shut and lock it, but then as more shots were fired. She knew she needed to get out of sight. Just as she dropped to her knees to climb under her desk, she heard the door to her office slam closed and lock. A moment later, standing behind her desk looking down at her was Miguel White holding a gun in his hand, covered in blood, and crying.

CHAPTER 42

Craig carried bags of groceries into the house. The song that was playing on the radio in the car still replayed in his head and he found himself humming it.

He set the bags on the table, and smiled as he looked at the photo on the refrigerator door.

To think, next summer would be completely different. He would opt to not do the summer session, if Rachel returned to work after her maternity leave, she'd have the following summer off, and the baby would be with them. The very thought of having an entire summer with his family made him giddy. Hell, just the thought that he was engaged to Rachel and they were having a baby made him giddy.

Pulling the gallon of milk from the bag, he turned to put it in the refrigerator just as his phone rang.

He shifted to pull his phone from his pocket as he put the milk on the shelf. Catherine's name came up on the ID. He let out a hum of confusion. Catherine never called him.

"Hey, Cath—"

"Tell me she's home," she cut him off. "Tell me she's home

with you right now," she rushed the words and her voice grew in pitch. "Is she home?"

"She's not here," he said closing the door on the refrigerator. "What's going on?"

"Active shooter at the high school," she shouted. "I'm headed over there. Miguel White."

Craig grabbed his keys and hurried back to his car. "They found him at his parents' house."

"He got away again. They think it's him."

Craig's body temperature increased and his heart raced so fast he thought he might pass out. "Cathy, she has to be okay."

"Shots fired near the front office. Injuries, but I don't know much more. She's in the goddamned building, Craig!" She was shouting now. "Her office is right inside the freaking office."

Pulling open the door of the car, he laid his hand on the roof and sucked in a breath. "Did you call her?"

"Of course I called her," she shouted again. "Craig!"

"She's okay," he said as he fell into the car. "We'll keep trying her. She's okay."

RACHEL LOOKED up into the wild, sad eyes of the young man who trembled before her. He'd come back for her, and there was no reason to think he wouldn't kill her.

"Miguel," she said softly as she watched tears stream from his eyes.

"Ms. Diaz, you need to help me. I need you to help me. Help me," he said over and over.

Rachel felt another wave of sickness swirl in her belly, but she had to will it down. She couldn't tempt fate and throw up on his shoes.

"Miguel, what's going on?"

"The voices. They're in my head again. I can hear them and they're loud."

Crouched under her desk, how was she supposed to talk to a teenage boy who was deeply distressed while he pointed a gun at her face?

"You're hearing the voices again?"

"They're trying to hurt me, Ms. Diaz. You gotta help me."

Rachel held her hands up so that he knew she couldn't harm him, and began to rise from under the desk.

Things had changed in the two decades since Columbine, and she knew her time with him was going to be brief. At any time, they'd come for him and that lock on her door wouldn't hold them off. They didn't just wait out active shooters anymore.

"Miguel, you need to put down the gun."

"No. Ms. Diaz, they said I need to use it."

"Who says?"

"The voices! Ain't you listening?" He shouted waving the gun.

Her hands trembled as she stood. "Okay, I understand. You're not taking your medicine?"

"Oh, no. They make me take that so they can control me."

"But doesn't it silence the voices?"

He seemed perplexed by her comment. "Yeah, but then they push people to do things. I don't wanna be pushed anymore. I need you to help me."

The sickness wasn't going to hold off much longer. Rachel pressed her hands to her stomach and took a breath.

"Miguel, I'm going to be sick. I'm pregnant, and I'm going to be sick."

His eyes went wide. "Oh, shit! They're going to kill you."

She had no choice now. Rushing to the corner of the room, she vomited in the trashcan while he shakily pointed the gun at her.

Taking another breath, she wiped her hand over her mouth and stood up.

For the first time, she took in the full sight of him. He couldn't be over one hundred and twenty pounds, and stood at least five-ten. Had they been starving him? If she rushed him she could easily knock him over, and he only held a hand gun. This wasn't the usual automatic weapon situation.

"I have some cookies on my desk. Would you like one. You look hungry."

His eyes widened and then narrowed. "I need help."

"I'm trying to help you. But you know as well as I do, they're going to break through that door any minute and we're both going to get hurt."

"You got a baby, they won't hurt you."

"They don't know about my baby, Miguel. Only you know."

That softened his eyes. "You married?"

"Not yet."

Now he shook his head and focused the gun on her again. "That ain't no good. My mama wasn't married either."

"We're getting married," she quickly added. "I've known him my whole life. He played basketball for my dad. My dad was a college basketball coach."

She knew if she kept him talking, maybe help would come.

"He's a good guy?" Miguel asked and the gun lowered slightly.

"He's the best guy."

"He better take care of you and your baby," he said with this voice firm now.

"Oh, he takes good care of us." She inched toward him. "Now, why don't you put down the gun. I'll open the door and we'll get some help for us."

He raised the gun again. "The voices say you're tricking me and I gotta take you out."

CHAPTER 43

There were crowds outside of the school when Craig pulled up and he had to run from the street to reach the barricade.

Two officers stopped his progress, pushing him back hard.

"Stand down, sir. You can't be here," one of the officers said.

"My fiancée is in there," he said urgently. "She's pregnant and in the office. You have to get her out of there."

The officer who still had a hand on his shoulder, locked eyes with him. "We're securing the scene. Students are being let out the other end of the building. Perhaps she's with them."

Craig shook his head. "She would have answered my calls by now. She's in the office."

He looked toward the front of the school and saw the busted windows.

"Craig," he heard Catherine's voice call to him.

The officer removed his hand as Catherine ran to him, gripping the front of his jacket. "He's got her. They're locked in her office."

He felt his knees go weak and they start to give out. The officer grabbed him again, and helped ease him to the ground.

Catherine lowered with him. "The kid came in with a hand gun. A goddamned hand gun. He shot out the windows. Injuries are only cuts and some debris. In fact, the office is empty, and it's just him and Rachel."

Was this supposed to make him feel better? A building with hundreds of people in it and it was going to be his fiancée and their baby who were the only victims?

She didn't deserve this. She'd been through enough. How much trauma could one person live through and continue on and want to help people?

Would they really stop him if he ran for the school to get her out?

Oh, who was he kidding? He was sitting on the ground because he couldn't even stand.

Tears rolled down his cheeks and he squeezed his eyes tight.

Coach, watch out for her. Get her out of there. I love them.

RACHEL WATCHED the barrel of the gun shake only inches from her face. She was going to get out of this, she swore it.

"Why you got that tattoo?" Miguel said shifting a glance to her arm.

Rachel looked down at the ocean scene and thought about the hours she'd spent getting that tattoo over the years to cover up her past.

"I have scars."

Miguel's lips twitched. "You in an accident?"

Pushing her shoulders back, she prepared to carry the weight of the truth. "No. When I was your age my brother killed himself and I found him." Miguel blinked hard and she thought he might be holding back tears. "I went down a dark path, Miguel," she made sure to use his name. "I started cutting myself, and I even tried to kill myself."

She turned her arm over to reveal the long line of coral in the design that hid the near fatal cut.

"My dad, the coach, he got me help," she continued.

The gun lowered slightly.

"Now you help people."

"I try to. I'd like to help you."

"They're loud," he cried now. "So loud."

Rachel stepped in closer and held out her hand. "Don't let them control you, Miguel. Put the gun down and let me help you."

His eyes searched hers and she knew she had him. He was going to surrender to her.

Miguel looked at the gun, and then at the desk. His finger still twitched over the trigger, but as he moved to lay it on the desk the door to the office flew open.

Miguel picked up the gun and fired toward the door.

Rachel screamed as shots came back their way, and she watched them hit Miguel, his body jerking with every hit.

And then she felt the burning sensation in her own body as she was thrust forward to the ground, falling right beside Miguel.

Blackness was closing in on her. Something was wrong, very wrong. Before the world went completely dark, she realized she'd been shot.

THE NOISE that rattled inside the school echoed outside. The crowd that had amassed took a collective inhale and then gone silent. Catherine had her arms wrapped tightly around Craig as they stood in the silent void.

It seemed like eternity, Craig thought, before people began to move, but then again, perhaps that was his own reality. Time was standing still, and he'd never felt more hopeless.

Sirens began, people moved, an ambulance hurried toward the school.

"He's down." Craig heard the words on a radio of a nearby officer. "There is one female victim."

His world went black, and all he heard was Catherine calling his name.

CHAPTER 44

As it was commonplace now, the media surrounded the crowd outside the school. An officer had loaded Craig and Catherine into his car, and with light on, he drove toward the hospital while Catherine held her jacket to Craig's bleeding head, which he'd cracked open on a rock when he'd fainted.

"It's okay," she kept saying, but it wasn't. And yet she'd repeat it again. "It's okay."

Craig heard the siren from the car, but also the siren from the ambulance that had raced up behind them to pass them.

His heart pounded. "She's in there."

Catherine batted her eyes as tears fell. "What are you talking about?"

"She's in that ambulance. They wouldn't be running if she weren't alive." He sat up taller. "Hurry. Get us to the hospital," he told the officer driving the car.

"I'll get you there. I'll see what I can find out on your fiancée too."

By the time they'd arrived at the hospital, media moved in on the entrance and were being pushed back by officers.

The officer driving the car pulled up behind the ambulance, and Craig watched as they unloaded the gurney and pushed it through the door.

The officer climbed out of the car and walked to his door, pulling it open. "That was her. She's heading into surgery right now. I don't know her condition. I don't know where she was shot."

Craig felt his world slipping from him again. "Please follow them," he begged the officer. "She's pregnant. They need to know she's pregnant."

He nodded and hurried into the entrance following the paramedic team.

Catherine helped Craig from the car and walked him into the emergency waiting area where they took his name, replaced Catherine's jacket with gauze, and took him back to a room.

They cleaned out the gash on the back of his head as Catherine called Hal, who was headed to pick up his mother and get to the hospital.

As they were beginning to staple Craig's wound together, the officer who had driven them to the hospital walked into the room with a somber looking doctor.

"I have news on your fiancée," the officer said.

Catherine moved to Craig and took his hand. If the doctor's eyes were a sign, things were bad.

"Your fiancée is in surgery right now. The bullet went through her shoulder and out through her back. There were no major organs hit, but her shoulder will need to be reconstructed."

Craig's jaw trembled and he couldn't get any words out.

Catherine gave his hand a squeeze. "She's alive?"

"She's alive and going to make a full recovery."

Craig batted his eyes against the tears that rapidly fell. "The baby?"

The doctor reached his hand out to Craig's shoulder, and Craig sucked in a breath.

"The baby's going to be okay too."

~

CRAIG SAT in the surgical waiting room with a throbbing headache holding Esther Diaz's hand as Hal paced down the hallway.

Rachel had been in surgery for hours, and every so often a nurse would come to them and give them an update.

Hal had made it very clear that they would not talk to the media that circled outside. Catherine, as a member of the county school department and close friend of the family, spoke to them on behalf of the Diaz family, and Craig felt as if that would buy them some time.

Alex and Bruce had both called and texted him to check up on her, and he knew Catherine and Hal's phones were flooded with well wishes and questions alike.

All Craig really cared about was seeing her face and holding her again. How many times could one person cheat death, he wondered.

Would this make her give up doing social work, or would it fuel her? Could he convince her to leave it all behind and just raise their baby?

As if he'd summoned him, the doctor walked into the waiting room and straight over to him and Rachel's mother. Hal hurried back into the room and stood with them.

"She's out of surgery and in recovery. It'll be just a bit before you can see her." He sat down next to Rachel's mother. "The bullet shattered her shoulder and went out her back. No vital organs were hit. She's going to need physical therapy, probably another surgery, and she'll have scarring."

They couldn't help but all chuckle wearily at that one. Craig wondered what kind of artwork she would choose for that.

"They'll send someone to talk to her about seeking professional help for what she went through, I have no doubt. But it looks like she has quite the alliance here."

"We're here for her," Craig said wrapping his arm around her mother's shoulders.

"They'll come for you when you can go back."

The doctor excused himself and Hal sat down. "She's a rock," he said. "No one else could have survived that."

Pride swelled inside of Craig. She was a rock.

CRAIG TOOK a walk while Rachel was still in recovery. He called the guys to tell them what had happened and what they could expect. Catherine had found him staring at vending machines and she put an arm around his shoulder.

"How's your head?" she asked.

Craig lifted his fingers to the staples at the back of his head. "Still attached. What a hero, huh? I faint and crack my head open."

"I can only imagine what was going through your mind. But she's going to be okay. The baby is going to be okay."

Craig nodded. "Yeah. It sure changes your perspective though. I can't help but wonder if she'll go back."

"I suppose it'll depend on the story she tells. I'm hearing she caught friendly fire, if you will. He didn't do this to her."

Lifting his eyes to meet Catherine's, he smiled. "I'm sure she was trying to help him until the very end."

"No doubt."

CHAPTER 45

Beeping sounds began to play in her ears, and Rachel tried to will her eyes open. There was light beyond her lids, but she struggled to see.

When she opened them slightly, the light grew brighter, but nothing focused. For a moment fear crept into her. The last thing she'd remembered was the world going black. Was this heaven? Had she really died in her office with Miguel?

"Rachel?" a soft voice called to her. "Rachel, sweetheart."

It was her mother. How was she hearing her mother?

She batted her eyes again, and each time it grew a little clearer.

"There she is," her mother said.

Rachel saw her mother's face now, and her mother smiled down at her. She hadn't died. She'd been saved, but where was she?

Another voice spoke, but she didn't understand. Then, Craig came into view next to her mother.

"Hey, sweetheart," he said softly and she focused on him.

She hadn't died.

Tears began to sting her eyes and she tried to bat them away. "Where..." it was the only word she could manage.

"You're in the hospital," her mother said. "You're going to be alright." She gave Rachel's hand a squeeze.

Her vision began to clear, and she noticed blood covering Craig's shirt. He hadn't been with her. How had he been shot? Was Miguel dead?

Then, her heart rate kicked up and the monitors beeped faster.

She looked up at Craig, but he smiled down at her.

"Baby..."

He exchanged looks with her mother. Something had happened to the baby.

Rachel's mother stood from the chair and Craig sat down, taking Rachel's free hand.

"The baby," he began and Rachel could feel her teeth begin to chatter. She searched his eyes for answers.

Craig pulled a picture from the pocket of his shirt and held it up for her to see. "The baby," he repeated. "The baby is doing just fine. She's strong, just like her mama."

"Our baby is okay?" Her voice was but a whisper.

"He's okay," he said smiling, changing the baby's sex, just as she'd done. "You're okay. It's all going to be okay."

Tears began to stream over Rachel's cheeks and her mother handed Craig a tissue. He wiped away her tears.

"You have blood on your shirt," Rachel said, her voice more steady. "Were you there?"

Craig lifted her hand to his lips and kissed her fingers. "I was there. Catherine and I were outside. When they said you'd been shot, I kinda fainted." He chuckled. "I hit my head on a very sharp rock. I have some staples and I owe Catherine a jacket."

Shot—she'd been shot. The word played as a trigger to the memory.

"Miguel?"

"He's dead, Rach."

She nodded. "He didn't shoot me."

Craig wiped a tear from his cheek. "You got hit in the cross-fire. You're the only person in all of this that got hurt, more than cuts from broken glass. Well, and Miguel..."

"He needed help," she cried. "He shouldn't be dead. He needed help."

"He made his choices, sweetheart. You have to think about that. You did what you could. Now you need to focus on you and the baby."

She realized then she couldn't move, as if her entire body were wrapped up. "What happened to me?"

"You were shot through the shoulder and it exited your back. Your shoulder was shattered. You had surgery, you'll need a lot of therapy, and they said you'll have scarring."

Rachel laughed. "I'll need new art."

Craig and her mother laughed too. "We already discussed that."

WHEN SHE COULD TAKE VISITORS, Craig arranged for everyone to see her. He was happy to see her eyes bright, even though she couldn't move much.

Toby had brought her flowers, and Bruce a box of fancy chocolates. Ray brought her pictures his kids had drawn, and Alex stood in the room making it clear that no one told him he was supposed to bring things.

Craig wondered if his ignorance of hospital culture made him more attractive, because Alex's arm was around Catherine's waist, and she didn't seem to mind having him that close.

Bruce had packed Craig a bag so he could stay with Rachel until she was released. And the bonus of her being in the hospital was that they continually checked on the baby, allowing them to hear the heartbeat and see the baby's image more often than they'd have gotten to.

When the room was quiet, and it was only them, Craig had moved to lay next to Rachel in the bed.

She caressed his face with her free hand, smiling at him with grateful eyes. "This changes everything, doesn't it?"

"Like what?"

"It'll be months before I can lift my arm into a wedding dress," she sighed.

"If you want the wedding dress, and that's an issue, we wait."

She let out a little laugh. "If we wait much longer, I won't be able to wear a wedding dress."

"They make wedding dresses for expecting mothers." He pressed a kiss to her lips. "Rach, I'm not going anywhere. So when you're ready to get married, we'll get married. This isn't going to hold me back from that." He laced his fingers with hers. "I sent up a prayer to your dad while I was in the parking lot to take care of both of you. He did that. He's still watching out for us."

Rachel rested her head against him. "I've been thinking about my job."

She felt him take in a breath. He had an opinion on it, she assumed.

"What were you thinking?"

"I can't give up, Craig. There are millions of people out there like Miguel and Theo who need people like me. He didn't go into that school to hurt me," she told him again. "He came for help."

"I'm not going to lie. I'd like you to be home and raise our kids. And that's not some sexist statement." He kissed her gently. "But I know you. The life you were given was meant to help people. You helped me. You helped others. And I know, by the way you tell the story, that you helped Miguel."

"I know I can't help everyone. I'm not a superhero. I get that. But I'm not out to cure everyone. I just want to help."

"I do think you're a superhero. And I am so grateful that you made me put my phone number in your phone at your father's funeral."

"Remember how I told you I seduced you for my first time?"

Craig laughed. "I'll never forget that."

"I had all intentions on doing it again if I had to. I was on a mission. I wasn't about to lose you from my life again."

CHAPTER 46

The dogs hurried up the driveway of Alex's new house. Rachel squeezed Craig's hand as they walked toward the back yard for the barbecue that Alex was having for Independence Day.

"Are you having second thoughts about selling to him?" she asked.

"Nah, but it was a damn good house. But when I'm finished with the bathroom at our house, and we decide on a color for the nursery, it'll be nicer than this house."

"We could paint the nursery purple or yellow or green. Neutral," she offered. "I mean, it'll have more than one baby in it over the years."

Craig stopped before they made it to the back of the house and turned her to him. "Four?"

"You want four kids?"

"For starters."

Rachel lifted her left arm to circle his neck, her right one still ached too much to lift it too high, even after a month of therapy. Rising on her toes, she pressed a kiss to his lips. "I suppose we should see how this one goes. I mean, I just got over morning sickness."

"Seriously, you think that's the biggest obstacle of this pregnancy? Need I remind you that you got shot and you've seemed to handle that just fine."

Rachel laughed. "All in a day's work, right?"

"Is that what your therapist has told you?"

"We both understand the risks. Humor helps."

The sound of someone clearing their throat pulled them apart.

Alex stood with a beer in each hand. "We could have just doggysat if the two of you had no plans to actually come to the party."

They both laughed and walked toward him, Craig's arm wrapped around Rachel's waist.

Alex handed Craig one of the beers. "Would you like a tour of my new house?"

Craig shook his head. "It's still raw man. Don't go putting salt in the wound."

Alex laughed. "I'd think you were serious if you didn't have one of the sexiest women in the world living in your house."

Rachel felt the heat rise in her cheeks. They'd all certainly moved past tip-toeing around the coach's daughter.

"Hey guys," Catherine's voice came from behind them and Rachel turned to see her walking up the drive with a bottle of wine. "I didn't know what to bring."

Alex's eyes softened when he looked at her. "That'll be just fine. We have so much food. I should have invited more people," he said as he and Craig walked toward the grill leaving Rachel and Catherine in the driveway.

"He invited you to his barbecue?" Rachel asked lacing her arm through her best friend's.

"I guess after all these years they've decided I'm not the enemy. Someone got to you, so I can let down my defenses."

Rachel laughed. "I think there's more to it than that. I think Alex is interested in you," she said softly as they neared the back yard.

"In me? No. If I remember right, when Craig disappeared, he came for you."

Rachel stopped walking. "He came to help me in a time of need."

"You don't think he just wanted a shot at you."

"I'm not going to say he didn't. It was ten years ago. But I think his motives were pure. And now, I think he's trying to get to know you."

Catherine looked toward the grill where Alex, Craig, and Ray stood. "Well, it's an interesting theory. But for the foreseeable future, I have a bridal shower to plan, and I know you're going to want my help planning your wedding." She smiled.

They walked to the back yard, arm in arm, and Rachel realized just how lucky she was. She not only had the man of her dreams by her side, she was carrying his baby, and her best friend's support never wavered.

And collectively, she was still surrounded by her family, and of course the team. Who could have known then, that they'd be as important years later.

While their friends drank their beers and spirits, Rachel sipped on her flavored water. She'd settled into a lounge chair because her shoulder hurt and her ankles had swollen in the heat.

"Are you doing okay?" Craig lowered next to her in the lounge.

"I'm fine. I am a little tired."

"We can go if you want."

She shook her head. "I don't want to pull you from all of this."

"I told him I wouldn't make a big deal out of him moving in and buying my house out from underneath me if he threw these kinds of shindigs every month."

Rachel laughed as she eased her head against his shoulder at the same moment the sky lit up from a few blocks over with the sound of pop bottle rockets and M-80s.

Rachel screamed and all heads turned.

Craig wrapped his arm around her tightly. "It's okay."

"No, no it's not. Get me out of here."

"They're just fireworks."

Her heart pounded in her chest and her hands shook. Craig must have had a change of heart because he stood, scooped her up in his arms, and carried her into the house and down to the basement.

THE LIGHTS WERE OFF, and the air was cool. Craig set her down on the couch and watched as she covered her ears with her hands and buried her face in his chest. The dogs had been right behind them as they hurried down the steps.

"Rach, are you okay?"

She shook in his hands and her breathing came in rapid gasps. The color in her skin had drained, and he wasn't sure what was happening to her. Clyde rested his head on her lap, as if he knew she needed him.

"Is something wrong with the baby?" Craig asked.

Rachel shook her head, but her body was telling him something completely different.

Another round of fireworks were set off and she screamed again.

Craig pulled her closer, now understanding what had happened, and wondering why he'd never considered that the festive celebration around them would sound violent in her mind.

She cried against his chest as he rocked her. It would be a long night—perhaps even week—he thought. Her entire world had changed, again, that fateful day that Miguel White burst through her office door.

CHAPTER 47

I t was nearly two in the morning before Rachel was ready to leave the confines of the basement. Every single one of their friends had come to them and checked on her.

Craig had put in a call to her therapist, who was able to calm her around midnight.

Now, as she walked up the back steps of the house that Craig had once lived in, she was weak and tired, and a little embarrassed.

The TV flickered in the living room.

Craig kissed her cheek. "I'm going to go tell them goodbye."

"I'll go with you," she said.

"Are you sure?"

Rachel nodded. "They need to know how grateful I am for their understanding."

He pressed a kiss to her lips. "You know that each and every one of them would do anything for you."

"I know that. My dad would be so proud of all of you."

"He'd be proud of you too. You know that right? Having something trigger trauma isn't a weakness."

Rachel smiled. "I know. I've had many calls from parents over the years that their child lost the battle against depression or drugs. It always takes me right back to finding Theo. But, then, I'll get a call or a letter from a student that says I changed their lives. Sometimes it's because I listened. Sometimes it's because I said something that gave them an ah-ha moment. I know, in my heart, Miguel was trying to capture that ah-ha moment, but his mind had betrayed him."

"You are so brave."

"No. I'm human and just like my father, I want to see everyone succeed." Rachel pressed her hand to his chest. "Now I know, fireworks will bring this back. If I hear a car backfire, I'll probably lose it. So I'll work on that. Don't expect me to watch any violent movies, though I don't usually go for those or emotional dramas. I'd rather everyone have a happily ever after."

"Is that what we're getting? A happily ever after?"

Rachel lifted her arms around Craig's neck. "That's what we're getting. Do you know how many times I wished for this?"

"Oh, I think I do."

"Do you know what else I've been thinking?"

Craig brushed a strand of her hair from her eyes and tucked it behind her ear. "What?"

"I don't want to wait until August to get married. I've been waiting to be married to you since I was fifteen. All of this only proves to me that life is too short to wait for anything."

"You don't want to wait?"

Rachel eased back. "Craig Turner, will you marry me, this week?"

Craig cupped her face in his hands. "Name the time and the place. You know I'll be there."

They both turned when they heard footsteps behind them.

"You guys doing okay?" Alex asked softly.

They exchanged gazes and Craig nodded. "I think we're doing just fine."

"Everyone is still up if you want to join us," Alex said.

Rachel nodded and hand in hand they walked to the living room.

Ray and Bruce sat in the recliners, while Toby sat on the sofa next to Catherine, who had curled up against him and fallen asleep with a blanket wrapped around her.

Rachel felt tears sting her eyes when she saw their friends gathered together, and she knew they'd all waited to make sure she was okay. Clyde and Rover had made themselves at home and were sleeping on the floor.

Catherine stirred and looked around the room. She shot up from the couch when she saw Rachel and Craig standing there.

"You're okay?" she asked hurrying to them, the blanket falling as she walked.

Rachel pulled her in and wrapped her arms around her. "I'm fine. I got triggered. I'll need to learn to deal with it."

Catherine tightened the hug. "You're so strong."

Again, Rachel wasn't sure their depiction of her was correct.

Alex stepped closer to them. "You guys can have one of the bedrooms if you want to stay. No need to go home in the middle of the night."

Rachel moved to him and kissed his cheek. He'd forever try to rescue her, she knew. "I think I'd like to go home. But thank you. And thank you for having us." She looked at Bruce, still in the recliner. "And thank you for letting me use your sofa all night."

"Not a problem."

Rachel looked back at Catherine. "We made some big decisions in the stairwell a few minutes ago," she said on a laugh and Craig wrapped his arm around her. "We'd like to get married next weekend. Are you free? Are you all free?"

Toby, Bruce, and Ray all stood and gathered around them now. She smiled when her thoughts went right to her father's huddle with the same men that surrounded her now.

"We're all free," Ray said, and everyone agreed.

"Then we'll have a wedding at my house next Saturday at three. Bring a dish to share," she teased and collectively they all moved in and hugged them.

EPILOGUE

R achel's mother had had a few words to say about the impromptu wedding. She would have liked her only daughter to have a big wedding with a mass and every relative there to share in the celebration. In one week, there wasn't time for a bridal shower or a bachelorette party. And they hadn't even been able to make table settings or buy a wedding dress.

But, after Rachel sat her mother down with her therapist, her mother's entire attitude shifted. Rachel needed those who she loved and trusted around her in her time of pure happiness, and after a few hours of tears, her mother understood and embraced the wedding.

She'd begged to make a fancy cake for Rachel and Craig, and if she couldn't have table arrangements, she wanted to sit with Rachel and Catherine and make small bags of candied almonds. That much Rachel could agree on.

"The guys are on their way over," Craig said as he buttoned up his shirt and tied his tie in the mirror. "My mom and sister will be here in fifteen minutes, and Catherine says the photographer has been taking pictures of the dogs."

Rachel laughed as she stood in her robe and took in the sight of Craig Turner, all six-foot-two-inches of him, shrugging on his suit jacket.

"You look so handsome," she said, gazing at him.

"I'm glad you think so. You're about to be stuck with me for life."

She laughed easily and moved to him as he adjusted his tie in the mirror. "There has never, ever been anything I want more."

Craig turned to her and took her hands in his. "I'm glad we're doing this today."

"Me too." She took a step back and untied her robe. "I want to show you something."

Craig chuckled. "Don't you think that should wait?"

Smiling, Rachel shrugged off the shoulders of her robe and turned her back toward him.

"Wow," he drew out the word. "When did you have that done?" he asked as she touched her back, just under her new tattoo.

"Thursday. And it's only Henna," she assured him. "But it's the design I want to get after the baby is born."

Craig examined the sun, which had been drawn over the scar where the bullet exited her body, and the moon that hung from a string below the sun.

"Tell me about it."

She turned toward him. "You are my sun," she said taking his hand and resting it on her taut stomach. "And this one hangs the moon."

His eyes grew damp. "That's beautiful."

"My mother went with me and she has a moon and from it hangs five stars."

"Five?"

"Me, Hal, Theo, my dad, and the baby."

Now a tear fell from his eye and Rachel wiped it from his cheek.

Caressing her face with his hand, Craig leaned in and kissed her. "I'll go get everyone organized. You come down when you're ready."

Rachel watched him walk out of the bedroom and close the door behind him. She let the robe fall to the floor and turned her back to the mirror. Looking over her shoulder she studied the new design that encompassed her most recent struggle and victory. In time it would be permanent, just as the art on her arm that covered her past.

Now, she was going to celebrate life, and go marry the man her father told her to never see again. Yet, at the same time, did everything he could to make sure Craig Turner succeeded too.

CRAIG STOOD in the back yard with their friends and family, the dogs with bow ties on their feet. When he saw Rachel walk out the back door, her hair in ringlet curls in a bright sundress, he knew his heart was about to burst.

She walked to him and took his hand. "I'm ready."

"So am I."

Everyone took a seat, and hand in hand, they walked to stand before everyone.

He'd promised he'd take care of the officiant, and he'd found the best one he could.

When Hal moved to stand in front of them, her father's Bible in his hands, Rachel immediately began to cry.

"You're going to marry us?"

"By the power of the internet and this guy asking me to be here for you," Hal said as he leaned in and kissed her.

"Surprised?" Craig asked as he took his handkerchief from his pocket and wiped her cheeks.

"I'm surprised."

Hal began the ceremony, and he'd added touches that made it

unique, like when he had them turn toward their family and each person in attendance said something beautiful to them about their union.

When it was Rachel's mother's turn to speak, she walked up to them and took each of their hands. "He knew. He knew the minute you walked into our house, and Rachel saw you, he knew you were part of our family. No matter what came in the years to follow, he loved you like a son. The only reason he forbade this was because you both needed to grow. Well, here you are. You're grown. You're wiser. You're having a baby. And you're so in love. He knew, and I know he gives his blessing."

Rachel fell into her mother's arms and Craig wiped away his own tears before Mrs. Diaz encouraged him to lean down so she could kiss his cheeks.

Hal cleared his throat. "The old man could always upstage us," he said and everyone laughed.

Rachel touched Craig's cheek. "I thought the day we buried my father, it was all about loss. I had no idea it was only the beginning."

Craig took her hand and kissed her palm. "And now we begin our forever."

We hope you enjoyed book one in the Funerals and Weddings
Series, *Something Lost.*
Please enjoy an excerpt from book two,
Something Discovered.

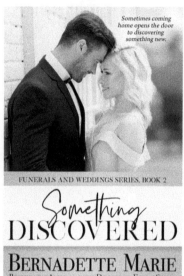

Sometimes coming
home opens the door
to discovering
something new.

FUNERALS AND WEDDINGS SERIES, BOOK 2

Something
DISCOVERED

BERNADETTE MARIE
BESTSELLING AUTHOR OF THE DEVEREAUX FAMILY SERIES

SOMETHING DISCOVERED

One of the perks of moving back to Colorado, Alex thought as he pulled his gym bag from his backseat, was being near *the team*. Who could have imagined when he'd flown out in February to attend their coach's funeral that he'd be back home for good, and that Sunday mornings would be for playing basketball with the boys again?

"Yo, Al," he heard his sister's voice from across the parking lot.

He watched as Sarah retrieved her bag and a ball and headed toward him. The additional perk was that he got to spend more time with his sister, too.

"I can't believe you still wear those sweatpants," he teased as she neared him wearing a ratty pair of University of Wyoming sweats.

"You know I never throw out treasures. Just think if I did, I'd have stopped talking to you years ago." She nudged him with her elbow.

"I can't decide if that's a compliment or a jab."

"Oh, hell, bro, I like you. Now, c'mon. I have a lot of caffeine in my veins and you and your friends need an ass-whooping."

And usually it was an ass-whooping they got if they were on a team opposite his sister. Though he and his old teammates had been hailed as some glory team in their time, none of them held a candle to Sarah.

Five years his junior, she'd grown up as his practice partner. Many late nights had been had in the driveway throwing free throws and layups. Perhaps she owed her skill to him.

They walked through the front door of the YMCA and toward the gym, where he could already hear his friends razzing one another.

Their voices carried down the hall, and it brought a smile to Alex's mouth.

He'd been gone since he'd graduated from college. Luck had given him a job in Philly, which eventually moved him to Jersey before he landed in Boston. Seeing the guys, who were brothers to him, was rare until last February when Alex had returned to Colorado for Coach's funeral. The five of them picked right back up where they'd left off.

As he turned the corner to the gym, he smiled. Craig was now married to Coach's daughter, and they were expecting a baby. Ray was a divorcée with two kids and it was his week with his kids, Alex noticed, when he saw Connor and Charlotte running through the gym bouncing a ball.

Toby tied up his fancy high tops, which Alex thought was out of character for the millionaire C.E.O. Other than his house and his car, nothing said the man was worth a lot. He was humble to the core.

Bruce, who lived in Alex's basement, in the house he'd bought from Craig when he'd decided to relocate back to Colorado, saw them walk through the door. And, as was the norm, he bee-lined for Sarah, bear hugging her and planting a noisy kiss on her cheek, before winking at Alex because he knew it drove him crazy.

Yes, this was his crew. He'd been back permanently for three months, and he'd fallen into a groove—they all had. As if the past decade since they'd graduated had never existed, they'd all melded right back into *the team*, and Alex was grateful to have them.

Toby looked up at Alex as he set his bag on the bench. "How's your mom doing?" he asked sincerely.

Alex smiled. "Great. After she recovered from her surgery, there's been no stopping her."

"That's good to hear." Toby stood up and swapped places with Bruce who sat down next to him.

"Do you bring your sister every week just to torment me?" he asked as he slipped his feet into his high tops.

"You know if you ever made a move on her she'd flatten you."

Bruce wiggled his brows. "She's in love with me. Always has been."

"In your dreams."

"She keeps me happy in my dreams." Bruce laughed and Alex shook his head. If Bruce ever laid a hand on his sister, he'd kill him. But for today, he'd take the ribbing.

Alex took his time putting on his shoes and just listening to his friends. When he'd finally looked up again, he saw Craig's wife Rachel walk through the door, and in tow was her best friend Catherine.

She caught Alex's casual glance, but whatever flashed in her eyes, it didn't give him warm fuzzies.

Catherine Anderson had always been a mystery to him. She was extremely protective of Rachel. That was understandable. Rachel had been surrounded by horny teenagers her entire life, since her father was a college basketball coach, and he had the team over often. Catherine had never much been one of Alex's fans, and he probably deserved that dishonor.

When Craig was out of the scene, after they'd graduated from college, Alex had moved in on Rachel. Though he'd been hopeful, it hadn't ended with him and Rachel in any kind of romantic partnership.

But in the last year, since Rachel's dad died and she'd fallen back in love with and married Craig, Catherine was around more, and they'd had their friendly exchanges. Hell, she'd even accepted his invite to his party over the Fourth of July.

Her eyes darted away, and he realized now he'd been staring. Well, no wonder the woman was creeped out by him. It was too bad too, he thought as he joined the others in the center of the court. Catherine had been on his mind a lot lately, and he'd like to try and mend that friction between them.

The teams were divided and Alex lined up for the tipoff.

Just as he jumped for the ball, his fingertips grazing it and sending it forward, he realized Catherine had stood from her seat to remove her coat and the ball flew right into her face.

MEET THE AUTHOR

Bestselling Author Bernadette Marie is known for building families readers want to be part of. Her series The Keller Family has graced bestseller charts since its release in 2011. Since then she has authored and published over forty books. The married mother of five sons promises romances with a *Happily Ever After always*…and says she can write it because she lives it.

Obsessed with the art of writing and the business of publishing, chronic entrepreneur Bernadette Marie established her own publishing house, 5 Prince Publishing, in 2011 to bring her own work to market as well as offer an opportunity for fresh voices in fiction to find a home as well. Bernadette is also an educator in the industry, offering workshops and speaking at conferences. In 2020 she was named the Independent Writer of the Year from the Rocky Mountain Fiction Writers.

When not immersed in the writing/publishing world, Bernadette Marie and her husband are watching their five hockey playing boys as well as running their family business. Bernadette is an avid Martial Artist with a second degree black belt in Tang Too Do, is a lover of a good stout craft beer, and might be slightly addicted to chocolate.